WHERE THE C]

F

ANDREA SMITH

Where the Crawfish Swim
by Andrea Smith
Meatball Taster Publishing, LLC.

Acknowledgments

Cover Design: Flirtation Designs
Editor: Erik Gevers
Formatting: Erik Gevers

Dedication

This book is dedicated to all of the brave men and women who work tirelessly to protect and secure our country. Specifically, agents of the U.S. Immigration and Customs Enforcement who deserve the respect of every American for what they do and the risks they take; agents of the Drug Enforcement Agency, *rank and file* agents of the F.B.I. and the members of Homeland Security.

Be careful out there.

Playlist for Where the Crawfish Swim

Heard It in a Love Song - The Marshall Tucker Band
I'm So Lonesome I Could Cry - B.J. Thomas
Somebody's Watching Me - Rockwell
Hungry Like the Wolf - Duran Duran
Wasted - Carrie Underwood
Undercover (Of the Night) - The Rolling Stones
Live Like You Were Dying - Tim McGraw
Flirtin' With Disaster - Molly Hatchet
Gimme Three Steps - Lynyrd Skynyrd
Only Here For A Little While - Billy Dean
Your Decision - Alice In Chains
Bleeding Out - Imagine Dragons
Feel Like Going Home - The Notting Hillbillies

Chapter 1

June 11, 2016

As soon as I pulled off the two-lane highway onto the gravel drive leading up to the Hatfield property, I sensed something was amiss.

The gate was standing ajar, which typically wasn't the way Vince Hatfield left it once he'd unlocked it for the day. I stopped my truck, got out and pushed the gate the rest of the way open, securing it against the fence with the metal hooks hanging from the post just for that purpose.

Back in my truck, I passed through the entrance, and took the first gravel lane to the right which circled around the property, passing three mobile homes. The first two were spaced about twenty yards apart, separated by a row of shrubs. The third trailer sat back from the others several hundred feet.

Vince Hatfield's cousin Ray, his girlfriend Denise, and her two kids inhabited the first trailer. The middle one was where Vince's daughter, Tammy Hatfield, stayed with her current boyfriend, James something-or-other, along with her daughter, Maddie and their newborn baby boy Barton.

The last one on the left was Harlan Hatfield's place, Vince's oldest son. A carport with a shed had been built to allow him more privacy from the others. Harlan liked his privacy when he wasn't partying.

Harlan's truck was parked under the carport and as I pulled up my truck behind it I saw that the window at the end of his trailer was wide open and the A/C unit had been pulled out and was now on the ground next to the metal skirting that surrounded the bottom of his mobile home. The screen on the top half of the open window had been cut as well. That was Harlan's bedroom window, I was pretty sure.

Strange.

As warm as it was, I couldn't imagine why he'd taken his window air conditioner out. And what was with the cut screen?

It was a little past seven. I was running a bit late. Harlan should have been up, sipping coffee on his front steps, smoking a cigarette while waiting for me to show. Just like he was every Saturday morning. Like clockwork.

The air was thick with silence at the compound. No Harlan, no music blasting from Tammy's trailer, no babies whining. The Hatfields were creatures of habit. Early risers, up and about even on weekends when most folks enjoyed the luxury of sleeping in a bit.

I jumped out of the truck and walked the few feet over to the wooden steps leading up to the deck that ran half the length of his trailer to the front door. Both the screen door and inside door were shut tight. I leaned in, listening for any sounds from inside to indicate Harlan was up and about. There was nothing. No sounds of a television, radio or Harlan bumping around inside.

Dead silence.

I pulled the screen door open and was about to knock when I saw it.

A reddish brown streak of something ran a wide swath down the center of the white steel framed front door. It looked like blood. I hesitated momentarily, and then pounded my fist on the door, my other hand trying to turn the knob at the same time. Nothing. The door was locked, and nothing indicated any activity inside.

My instincts instantly went on high alert. I let the screen door slam shut and returned to my truck, backing out and heading up the curved drive that led to the main house.

I wasn't about to step into Harlan's place without Vince or his wife being with me. This family was clannish. Trusted few people, and stayed to themselves for the most part. I wasn't about to force Harlan's door open until I had somebody with me if for no other reason than to witness whatever was behind that damn door.

As I rounded the bend, I saw Vince's truck parked in the usual spot. I was relieved although a bit surprised he hadn't left for work yet. He was generally gone before seven, meticulous about leaving the main gate open for me, knowing I'd arrive around seven.

His wife's SUV was right next to his truck, and his teenage son Darrel's new Mustang parked next to hers.

Vince's two pit bulls were out on the porch, wandering around the front door unleashed.

That never happened.

The dogs stayed mostly inside, obviously bred and trained for protection. To see them pacing on Vince Hatfield's front porch, scratching at the screen door, was in no way typical behavior for the dogs.

I jumped out of my truck and headed up the steps of the front porch, noticing immediately that the door to the main house was ajar. I cupped my hands and peered through the screen door, the dogs whining beside me as I did.

There were no sounds from within the house, and the interior door wasn't opened far enough to allow me to see anything. I opened the screen door, and pushed the interior door wide, slowly stepping inside the house.

It was as quiet as a tomb . . . which made sense, because after I'd taken several steps from the narrow hallway into the front room, glancing around at the carnage, I realized it was indeed a tomb. I pulled my cell from the pocket of my jeans and called 9-1-1.

Afterwards, my brain in a fog, I left the crime scene, to go outside as instructed and made sure to get the dogs on their chains before law enforcement arrived.

I dug my cell phone out again and called Harlan. I knew he wouldn't answer, but I let it ring and ring until it finally went to voicemail. "This is Harlan. Leave a message and if I feel like it, I'll call your ass back."

Beep!

I ended the call and quickly hit the other number I needed to call. When answered, I spoke quickly, "We've got trouble in Briar County. Better get someone down here stat."

Call ended.

I relived what I'd seen inside. I hadn't gone further into the house once I saw the two blood-soaked bodies of Vince and Darrell on the floor of their living room.

Vince's eyes were open, but they had that dead blank look in them, no longer able to blink, his most likely last vision was that of his murderer. I assessed the rest of his body. His face and neck were bruised, a gag placed over his mouth.

His arms and legs had been hog-tied. His shirt had been ripped open. I could see the bruises and some strange half-moon welts that covered his stomach and chest. It looked as if he'd been tortured and maybe kicked with steel-toed boots. But the strangest thing was that his body was framed by hundred dollar bills stacked neatly around him. Somebody had taken his time in doing this, displaying him surrounded by money. But why? What was the message?

It was more difficult to look at Darrell. The kid was only sixteen for Chrissake! He was slumped on the floor in the doorway leading from the kitchen to the living room. It didn't appear as if he'd endured the beating or torture his father had received.

More than likely he'd walked in on the fray; he was wearing pajama pants and a wife beater tee, and looked to have been shot in the head close range. There was a path of blood and brain matter on the white wooden doorjamb, most likely left as the boy slid down against it to the floor after being shot.

I couldn't erase those images from my mind. Maybe I never would. I leaned against the tree, closing my eyes trying to wrap my mind about what possibly could have gone down last night or earlier this morning with the Hatfields.

There was more carnage to be found. I felt it with every fiber of my being. But there was no way I was going any deeper into that crime scene. I'd known that without having to be told by the dispatcher to leave the house immediately and await the authorities.

In the distance, I could hear the shrill echoes of multiple sirens getting closer. And just before the first county deputy's car pulled off the road to head up the drive, I leaned over and puked my guts out behind a tree.

Chapter 2

Six months prior . . .

Dalton Edwards drove his pick-up truck along the two-lane, winding country road, turning his head intermittently to take a quick glance to the left or right in an effort to take in the countryside of this rural sparsely populated county.

Southern Ohio was new to him. It certainly bore no resemblance to Columbus, the state capitol, and where he'd made his home for the past three years. A modern city where restaurants, stores, entertainment, and major interstates wrap themselves around the city like one would expect in a metropolitan area.

This county in Southern Ohio was completely different, and only a mere seventy miles away. At the foothills of the Appalachian Mountains, east of "the ridge" which locals referred to it as, Briar County was a place where farming and poverty were the major sources of income.

Small towns dotted the roads here and there, and Dalton couldn't help but notice the contrast of rural living that was apparent in this particular area of the county.

Dalton passed by majestic log homes that were sitting atop rolling hills, flanked by uniformly spaced evergreens and paved circular driveways.

But in the blink of an eye, he rolled past rusted trailers with clotheslines out front, dilapidated vehicles up on blocks. There was a dotting of clapboard shacks heated by wood stoves, smoke curling out of crumbled chimneys with outhouses placed a few yards behind the structures.

Many of the homes had discarded bikes and children's toys strewn about the yards, and even the soft blanket of snow did little to hide the obvious poverty of many, and the sprinkling of wealth mixed in between.

Dalton was more than a bit awestruck by the flagrant contrast in this rural community. But he'd been warned by his boss, "You're gonna love Appalachia, Edwards," Alan Munson had chided. "It'll be a nice break from the same ole, same ole. Think of it as a learning experience. And don't fuck it up."

Dalton hadn't been fooled for one second. This was a punishment. He knew. Munson hadn't appreciated the fact that Dalton had been tapping his oldest daughter, Tiffany, every chance he got. But when Dalton had broken things off with her, he had no idea just how far Alan would go to make his life miserable.

Until now.

All he could do was make the best of it. Do his job, ingratiate himself with the community. See just how much money was to be made in Briar County.

He was no farmer, that much was obvious. But he knew there were other, less honest ways to make tax free money in the area and that was what he'd been tasked to do.

There was money to be made according to Alan. "Get your fingers in it, Edwards. Earn your pay. Your new contact will be in touch with you shortly."

∞

Dalton Edwards was less than happy with the job he'd landed in Briarton, a town of about twenty-five hundred residents, but job opportunities were slim, and flipping burgers weren't his thing.

Apparently, shoveling horse and pig shit, mopping down stalls and changing out straw and hay had become Dalton's newest career. But, since his instructions were to blend in with the community, this gig was as good as any he figured.

Dalton had seen a "Part Time Help Wanted" posting at a local diner upon arriving in the small burg. He immediately called the number, and shortly thereafter, he was hired by Virginia McCoy, a well-known figure in the community.

She was a crusty old broad, looked to be in her seventies, but it didn't take her five minutes to lay out the job description and tell him if he proved to work out, he'd have a job.

"I don't take to slackers," she had explained. "You'll work hard and answer to my son, Duel. He's the ranch foreman. I do the hiring. He does the firing. People around here know I'm a no nonsense type of gal, and Duel's no different. Honest work gets you fair pay."

Dalton nodded as she continued, "You'll work three days a week. I hire part-time only so I don't get forced into paying benefits. It's better for my business that way. You look to be in good shape physically, and that's what I need. You best like animals, because you'll be working with lots of them. You do like animals don't you Mr. Edwards?"

"Oh yes...yes Ma'am," he'd replied, "Love them. No problem there."

"Good. I presume you have a valid driver's license, young man?"

Dalton had been a bit taken aback by that question being the job she'd outlined would be as a ranch hand.

"Yes, Ma'am," he'd replied.

"Because your duties will also include miscellaneous errands, including picking up rent checks from tenants on my various properties. Will that be a problem?"

Dalton couldn't think of a better way to meet more people in the community, maybe strike up some friendships. "Not at all, Ma'am," he replied with a smile.

"Good. You need to know some of my tenants are dead beats who'll give you a sob story when they can't pay. You'll need to be able to handle them in a manner that produces the monies owed me. Is that understood?"

"Absolutely."

So much for cultivating friendships, he thought to himself. He'd be known as the county bone breaker. Shit.

"Fine. Now if I might see your driver's license and along with your social security number we can complete your application for employment."

And that was all there was to Dalton landing a job at the East Fork Ranch, a two thousand acre spread outside of Briarton.

Dalton quickly learned that the McCoy family was well known for the lucrative horse breeding of miniature horses, Vietnamese potbelly pigs, peacocks, and other exotic animals.

From what he could tell, the old woman had an extremely lucrative business going on with the ranch, and a host of other income-producing entities.

Apparently, she and her old man, who'd passed away some years before, had built their empire in this county. Everybody knew her.

Some worshipped her, others not so much. Dalton wasn't sure what that was all about, but for the time being, his only mission was to acclimate himself with the community, and in this community the name McCoy carried a whole lot of clout.

Virginia McCoy had made it clear to him that his job entailed a variety of duties and he was to keep his personal life in town and not on her ranch.

"I've no time or stomach for gossip or drama," she'd explained. "Too darn many people already in my business around these parts. Take my advice, Dalton, keep your nose clean and watch out for snakes. There's plenty of them slithering around Briar County. And, you'll need your own place. I don't have my help bunking here. Had too many bad experiences with that."

There were several other part-time ranch hands. Apparently the only full-time help on the payroll were family members. Her son Duel, and grandsons Grant and Brant. Duel and his wife, Sally Jo had their own house down the road on McCoy land. Her grandsons lived elsewhere.

Dalton wasn't sure about the grandsons. They seemed to live in their own little "entitled world." For as no-nonsense as Virginia McCoy was, the old woman apparently had a soft spot for her grandchildren.

From what Dalton could tell, everything was in place to ensure they had money without breaking a sweat to earn it; a remote place to live and do their "own thing" whatever that happened to be, and plenty of toys to keep them entertained.

Cars for the demolition competitions; roosters for the cock fighting, and probably as much weed as they needed to party "like it was 1999."

Only it wasn't 1999.

It was 2016 and things around Briar County seemed to be tense and pretty secretive. Almost clannish, if Dalton had to choose a word for it.

Yeah, there was definitely illegal shit going down in this county, but nothing earth shattering. At least that he could tell so far.

For the first time, Dalton wondered just exactly how much Intel the DEA really had about the goings on in Briar County. He got the feeling that it was more than what his superiors suspected.

WHERE THE CRAWFISH SWIM

Chapter 3

Dalton had settled himself into life in Briar County. For most it was a simple life. Not one that he had ever been accustomed to, having grown up in upstate New York where the hustle and bustle of everyday life set a pace which would make the heads of people in this neck of the woods spin like crazy.

Briarton was laid back. People were friendly on the surface anyway. Families lived close to one another. People attended church regularly, looked out for their neighbors but kept their secrets cloaked in armor.

They were a protective bunch, and while everyone treated him with friendly courtesy, he was still an outsider and he had a feeling it would be like that for a long spell, as a local might put it.

His work on the ranch provided some interesting insight into just how much of a powerful figure Virginia McCoy was in this small community. She could be a tough taskmaster, but it was clear she had a sharp business mind, and was nobody's pawn.

Virginia was active in her church, and ran several benevolent organizations in the community. One such organization was a group home for mentally disabled adults that she had founded years ago. Her daughter-in-law, Sally Jo, was the paid director of the non-profit organization.

Virginia's son, Duel, pretty much ran the operations of the horse ranch. Dalton reported directly to him for his daily assignments beyond the usual barn maintenance.

Duel McCoy was mid-forties, tall and lean with dark, slicked-back hair, and piercing blue eyes. His arms were muscular and sported a farmer's tan, ultimately a result of his working outside on the ranch. Not a particularly handsome or savvy individual, but Duel knew his stuff where the horses were concerned.

Dalton had been fascinated when he first laid eyes on the miniature horses. "They aren't much bigger than a Great Dane," Dalton had said, "What's the purpose?"

Duel had laughed at Dalton's apparent ignorance of these breeds. "They're show horses, mostly. And, of course, we breed them and sell them as well. Most people like them because of their size. None of ours are more than thirty-three inches. Anything over thirty-four inches doesn't qualify for AMHA registration. That's important to get the best sale price. Hell, boy, we have people from Beverly Hills, California with their own reality shows fly out here to buy these babies for their kid's birthday party," he finished with a wink.

Dalton got the reference and chuckled, "Well are they all for sale?" he questioned. "Some of them look like they've got some age to them."

"Yeah, well those are ones we just can't part with. They're like family to us."

∞

Dalton had just finished up in the horse barn when he saw a truck coming down the long driveway, past Virginia's sprawling house, and then veering over to where Duel was mixing various grains in the huge feeder for the horses. The truck skidded to a stop, the tires spitting gravel up in a cloud of dust all around them.

It was one of Duel's sons, the youngest, Brant. And it was obvious to Dalton, the dude was pissed as he jumped from the truck and approached his father.

Brant McCoy was mid-twenties, just a couple of years younger than Dalton. He was a smaller version of his father, not nearly as muscular, in fact, downright scrawny in comparison.

According to bits and pieces Dalton had picked up around the community, Brant also managed a hunting and fishing recreational business owned by Grandma McCoy. Dalton wasn't familiar with the place, but would've bet his paycheck that Brant didn't break a sweat on much of anything he did. He drove a ranch-owned truck, as did his older by a year brother, Grant. Entitled fucks, with twin names and cloned personalities.

Grant worked at the ranch a few days a week as well, nothing that required hard labor. According to Duel, Grant's job was managing the breeding contracts, sales and website for the East Fork Ranch. Paperwork stuff as Duel described it, boasting that his oldest had a knack for the techy stuff that he lacked.

The brothers lived in the next county over on a pretty big farm where Dalton was sure they busied themselves with whatever entitled hobbies that caught their fancy at the moment. Virginia bragged about them constantly, telling anybody who cared to listen about their genius with restoring racecars and dirt bikes for important people, and being so very talented both mechanically and technically. Frankly, Dalton couldn't see it, but then, he really only saw them in passing.

Dalton's ears perked up while he busied himself sweeping the floor of the barn near the entrance so he could hear what had Brant all riled up.

"She's a fucking bitch! I swear to God, she's on my last nerve, Dad! She wants more money. She says we can afford it. I'm sick to fuck of giving the bitch any more money when she's fucking that low life loser who hasn't got shit to his name! She's trying to hold my daughter from me. Fuck her!" Brant was definitely in a tirade. And a very loud one at that.

"Calm your ass down, Brant," Duel hissed, glancing over at Dalton. "We don't put family business out in the public like that boy."

"Yeah, yeah," Brant growled. "But we need to talk Daddy."

"Dalton, can you finish this up for me?" Duel hollered over to him.

"Sure thing," Dalton called out, heading towards the pasture.

"Go on up to the house, Brant. I'll be up in a minute. And cool down before you go into Granny's house. She doesn't want to hear all that cussing. We'll sit down and calmly discuss it in private. Now go on."

Brant stalked over to where he'd left his truck with the door hanging open and climbed back into it. The tires tossed gravel as he peeled out and headed back up the lane pulling around to the front of Virginia's house.

"I swear," Duel said once Dalton started scooping the grain into the bin, "sometimes I have to wonder just what my boy was thinking when he laid with that girl."

Dalton remained silent. He knew that Duel and Sally Jo had a granddaughter they doted on constantly. It was their only grandbaby and they made no secret of spoiling the little girl. But that was the extent of what he knew about the situation.

"I got some family business to tend to at the moment. So go ahead and finish up here and then you can go on home for the day."

"No problem," Dalton replied. "I'll see that everything's done. See you tomorrow, Duel."

Chapter 4

Dalton knew that he was quickly becoming part of the community. He knew that after his day working with Duel. It was the first time he'd gone with him on a "collection run," as Duel had termed it.

He'd just finished cleaning the stalls when Duel came into the barn.

"Hey Dalton, ready to go on your first collection run so you can see how it's done?"

"Collection run?"

"Yep. You need to go with me and see how we deal with squatters. When they fall behind on their payments, that's what they become . . . squatters. And if I have to go out there personally, it means business. Either put out the cash or get out."

On the way to the purported squatters residence, Duel filled Dalton in as to the specifics. "As you've probably gathered already, lots of hard-working people living in poverty, Dalton. Mama has multiple parcels with mobile homes that she sells on land contract.

"You see, for the most part the folks who buy them don't qualify for mortgage loans. If they pay off the land contract, she deeds over the property to them. If they don't, well, she gives them a chance to catch up. One chance only. The Driscolls are two payments behind. If they don't pay up today, they're served with a 15 Day Demand. Be prepared. Sometimes it can get nasty."

An hour later, Dalton reflected on Duel's choice of words. Nasty didn't do it justice.

Elroy Driscoll was a man in his sixties. He was on a walker after having had major back surgery. He had been working as a mechanic out of the garage located on his small piece of property, but hadn't been able to bend, lift, or squat since the surgery. His wife, Ida, worked as a cook at one of the local schools, but her pay hardly covered anything beyond the utilities, groceries, and phone bill.

When Duel had approached the old man with a notarized copy of a 15-Day Demand, Dalton could see the desperation on Elroy's face. "You can't be serious," he said after reading the document. "There's no way I can come up with $1800 in just fifteen days, Duel. Besides, I'm only two months behind, that's only $1200..."

"If you'd read your land contract like you should have done before signing it, Elroy, you'd recall the daily late charge that accumulates. I figured you were smart enough to do the math," Duel replied icily.

Elroy's shoulders sagged in defeat. "But . . . how can you expect me to come up with that kind of money when I can't even work right now?"

Duel shrugged. "Sell your mechanics tools. Seems like they might be worth that much."

"If I do that, how can I continue in the trade once I'm able to work again?" Elroy pleaded.

"Not my problem, Elroy. You've been served. You've got fifteen days. Dalton here will be by at the end of it to collect or present your eviction notice. Figure it out."

Dalton felt like a total piece of shit having witnessed what transpired in the collection process of Virginia McCoy's land contract holdings. He didn't have the stomach for it, and he wanted no part of it. This whole gig at the McCoys wasn't panning out for the purpose he'd been sent to Briar County for in the first place.

Once back in the truck, he told Duel as much. "Hey man," Dalton said, "I enjoy drawing a paycheck Duel, and to be honest, there's not much I wouldn't do to earn my pay around here. But shaking down an old man? That's just not my thing. If that's going to be a job requirement, maybe I should look for something else."

Duel chewed on a toothpick while he considered what Dalton had just said to him. Maybe he should shit-can Dalton, but so far, the guy had proven to be a good worker. Kept to himself. Didn't run his mouth. Showed up on time and didn't slack off like some of the others.

"Tell you what, Dalton," Duel finally said, "Maybe there is something else you can help out with. You mind working a once-or-twice-a-month gig for me? It's a third shift task, but pays pretty good. Interested?"

"Maybe. Tell me more."

ANDREA SMITH

Chapter 5

Dalton Edwards heard his cell phone vibrating on the nightstand next to his bed. His hand shot out in the dark, feeling the surface until he found it, bringing it up to his ear as his finger pressed the screen that would magically connect him to his supervisor. Nobody else ever called this number.

No one else knew it.

And it changed monthly.

"Dalton," Duel's voice barked, "It's time."

Dalton surged out of his bed, and his hands searched in the darkness to find the lamp switch. He fumbled with it, and finally switched it on, illuminating the room.

It was pitch dark in this neck of the woods. And being a city boy, it was a bit of a shock to look up into the sky and see the stars sprinkled against the black velvet backdrop of night. That was, of course, if there was no cloud cover.

"Hey, you there?" Duel McCoy's voice was terse and impatient.

"How much time do I have?" Dalton asked, already grabbing the pair of jeans he'd tossed carelessly over the guest chair at the hayseed motel he'd been staying at for the last four months.

"ETA is less than thirty minutes. Get your ass in gear and get up to the ridge."

Dalton fastened his jeans, pulled the black sweatshirt out of the closet and within ten minutes, he was pulling his dark blue pick-up truck up the dirt lane, with only his parking lights guiding him up to the top of the crest, where the others would be waiting or following him in momentarily.

The digital clock on his radio read 3:12 a.m. as he shut the engine off and exited the vehicle to start working.

By the time he reached the clearing, Duel was already unfastening the hardware that kept the artificial turf in place. Dalton jogged over to where he was, helping him to disengage the locks.

"Grab the winch, and lock the end hooks into place," he snapped. "Where the hell is Hatfield?"

Dalton had no clue where Harlan Hatfield was, but his best guess would be that he was sleeping off a moonshine binge in somebody's trailer. He wasn't as dependable as Duel liked.

Not like Dalton.

Together they got the hooks locked in, and just then, Harlan hightailed it over the ridge, and rolled the pulley over to where the other two men stood, connecting it to the winch.

Dalton and Harlan started operating the pulley handle, the first few turns of the spindle were always a bitch until they got the swing of it. The weight lessened as the twenty-four hundred feet of specially designed artificial foliage rolled back, wrapping itself around the wide spindle. Once done, it exposed the asphalt strip where the Cessna would be landing in a matter of minutes.

"I got this, I got this!" Duel growled, once the momentum had hit stride. "Go on over and flip the switch, Dalton. There'll be hell to pay if they gotta circle before landing."

Dalton jogged over to a large oak tree about twenty yards back from the clearing, and reached inside a hollowed-out knot, his groping fingers found the switch and pushed it upward.

Immediately, the landing lights that were flush with the runway on both sides of the asphalt strip illuminated in the night, but not enough to draw the attention of anyone other than the pilot who would be looking for them soon.

Minutes later, they all heard the steady hum of the Cessna engine grow louder as it made its initial approach over the ridge in the quiet darkness of the night.

The beauty of this area was that no one was ever out this way. It was no-man's-land. Perfect for the business they all found themselves in.

Good pay.

Good hours.

No taxes.

The men stood back as the Cessna 172 Skyhawk made a smooth landing in the dark night. They continued to wait where they stood as the two occupants cleared the craft, and then Duel fired up his ATV with the covered trailer attached and headed down the strip to load the goods and the men into it.

That was Harlan and Dalton's signal to leave. They weren't permitted to go any closer to the aircraft, and they were to take one of the vehicles and go to wait in the parking lot of a church about three miles down the road until further notice.

This was only the second time Dalton had been on this special gig, as Duel had phrased it. The last time they'd had about a two hour wait, for which they were instructed to stay together until Duel called one of them on their disposable phones (as both men had taken to calling them) and instructed them that all was clear to come back to the ridge and put things back into place.

The plane was always gone when they returned. In fact, seldom did they ever hear it leave, this particular property was no more than ten or fifteen acres, but it was atop a ridge and not good for much of anything. There weren't any roads going through it so it seemed to be a fairly discreet and secure setup.

Once they finished, Duel would hand each of the men five hundred bucks, which would carry them over until the next delivery. Generally, that would be in another two to three weeks. Not bad money for a couple hours' work and keeping their respective mouths shut.

Dawn was breaking as Harlan and Dalton headed down the hill to where their vehicles were parked.

"Hey, Dalt," Harlan said, chewing on a toothpick he'd had in his mouth all night. "How much money you think those dudes drop on Duel for this?"

Dalton turned back over his shoulder to look at him. "Have no clue. Why don't you ask him?"

He scoffed and kicked at some of the dry, dead leaves they were traipsing through. "I ain't crazy, man. Just thought maybe he'd shared that information with you, that's all. You two seem pretty tight."

Dalton stopped in his tracks, waiting for Harlan to catch up. "Hell, you've known Duel all your life, dog. I've just been around a few months. What the hell are you talking about?"

He shrugged. "Treats you with more respect, that's all."

Dalton tossed Harlan a sidelong glance. He wasn't sure what Harlan meant by that, but it definitely smelled like some sort of a fishing expedition.

"I didn't notice," Dalton replied briskly. "We ain't exactly in the same social circles if you catch my drift. I'm the newcomer here. All I do is what I'm told to do, when I'm told to do it, and then collect my pay which is pretty damn good. Especially in these parts. What? You wanting a raise, Harlan?"

Harlan spit the toothpick out, and shoved his hands in his pockets. "I wouldn't turn one down. Seeing how Duel lives and all. Got all that land, all those exotic animals, those fine cars and trucks. Heard he's got a new fishing boat too, did you know that?"

"No, Harlan. I didn't know that. But like I said, I don't socialize with him. I only work for his family. Go to their ranch a few days a week and even there I try my best to keep to myself. I was warned before I was hired to keep my social life off the ranch. Virginia McCoy doesn't like personal drama. You gotta remember, I wasn't born and raised around here. It's not like I don't want to make friends, but the McCoys are kinda outta my league."

"I can't fault you for that, being an outsider and all. Yeah, the McCoys are a different bunch, but hey, you gotta get a social life. How about you and me go out for a beer sometime? As they say in these parts, 'You're only a stranger for as long as you wanna be.'"

"Is that right? Well, sure, I guess. Might as well get out and about."

"Cool. Maybe tonight since we both got money burning holes in our pockets, yeah?"

Dalton smiled. "Sure, sounds good. Just tell me where."

"You still staying at that old roach motel up the road?"

"Yep."

"Pick you up at nine. We can shoot darts or maybe play some pool. I'll show you some of the hot spots around here."

"See ya then, Harlan."

Dalton certainly wasn't going to miss an opportunity to do some socializing. It was one of the best ways to meet more locals, gain friendships and trusts, and ingratiate himself with this close-knit, almost cult-like community he'd come to call home - for the time being anyway.

Billy Ray Jensen had just finished night fishing. He'd packed up his gear, and tossed the two Scioto River flatheads he'd caught into the cooler. He'd hoped for more catfish, being it was March and all, but at least he wasn't going home with nothing.

Truth be told, he might've done a bit better if he hadn't fallen asleep on the riverbank for Lord knows how long. He chuckled to himself as he headed up the well-worn path to where his truck was parked on the side of the road.

It was just breaking dawn as he loaded everything in the back of his pick-up, and slid into the driver's seat, turning on the engine. There was a distinct chill in the air.

As he waited in the cab, putting the heat on high to get his blood flowing again, he happened to notice two black Suburbans pass by him.

Strange, he thought to himself. SUV's weren't a rarity in this neck of the woods, but two of them, same model, same color, this time of the morning was a bit odd. Not only that, but he now recollected this wasn't the first time he'd seen them in the area.

WHERE THE CRAWFISH SWIM

The last time he'd gone fishing, he'd seen them too. Only that time, they'd been turning onto the road from the Appalachian Highway. This time, they were on their way out of the county, it appeared.

He glanced into his rearview mirror and noted that one turned right, heading east towards West Virginia, while the other made a left, heading west towards Cincinnati.

He didn't give it much more thought. He was, after all, anxious to get home to get his fish cleaned for this evening's supper. Besides that, as long as nobody bothered him, he wasn't the sort to give a lot of thought to others that might pass through the area.

Only he couldn't quite put it all out of his mind. Those Suburbans had come from further on up the road. Only two farms on this particular road, Billy Ray's land, and the Hatfield land. They bordered one another.

Hell, the Hatfields had lived in the county for generations, just like the Jensen family had. Billy Ray had gone to school with Floyd Hatfield. A great farmer, and honest as the day was long.

The same unfortunately couldn't be said for his offspring. For whatever reason, his only son had always been a bit reckless. Not one to take any particular interest in farming or ranching.

Still, when Floyd passed, his son Vince had inherited the farm, with all of the accompanying acreage. Floyd's wife, Vince's mother, had fled the coop when Vince was just an adolescent. Country living just wasn't her thing or so she had told Floyd.

Billy Ray wasn't exactly sure what Vince Hatfield had going on with the property. He didn't farm it the way his father had, but he seemed to spend a lot of time acquiring old beater cars that he and his son converted into demolition vehicles for competitions.

Vince had a new wife, Mary Beth, a teenage daughter who the locals referred to as being rather "round heeled," his oldest boy Harlan, who was in his mid-twenties, and his youngest boy, sixteen year old Darrell who according to Billy Ray had that whole entitlement thing going on.

Billy Ray wasn't impressed with any of them, truth be told. The whole clan spent an inordinate amount of time with those old beaters getting them road-worthy for the demolition events, and other than that, he wasn't sure what all they did for a living.

There wasn't a lot of money in derby events, but then, Billy Ray suspected the Hatfields had other means of making ends meet. Or so the local gossip had it.

He wasn't going to let it concern him. He'd retired five years ago from the sheriff's department over in Scioto County and he didn't miss it one little bit. The politics; the ass-kissing to the higher ranks, and even the payoffs for certain detectives to 'look the other way' had pretty much soured Billy Ray on the whole law enforcement career choice.

He was much more amenable to living his life in his closed off bubble. Evil was here to stay. Goodness had lost the fight.

WHERE THE CRAWFISH SWIM

Chapter 6

Dalton Edwards had showered, shaved, and polished his black boots all before he heard the sound of Harlan's horn out front of his motel room. He grabbed his jean jacket, pack of smokes, and headed out of his room into the cool, March night.

It was a clear night, and he glanced up to check for stars. Yep. There they were. He'd considered taking the time to lie out in the bed of his truck some night when the skies were clear and attempt to count the stars just to see if he could. Dalton liked challenges. They were his poison.

He climbed into the passenger seat of Harlan's pick-up, and immediately realized that Harlan's sprucing up evidently consisted of dousing himself with a cheap men's cologne and a fresh toothpick. He had managed to slick back his dirty blond hair into a stubby ponytail.

"Ready to par-tee?" Harlan whooped, backing his truck out with a squeal. "First stop, 'Pike's Peak.' Have you been there?"

"Naw, haven't been anywhere, truthfully."

"Oh man, well then this is gonna be a real treat, hear? The best, and I mean the fucking best moonshine to ever cross your lips, dude."

"I'm not much into moonshine, Harlan."

"How do you know until you try some?"

"I just know."

"Where the hell are you from, boy? Persnicketyville?" He laughed at his own question and then slapped his thigh. Dalton wondered if Harlan had already started with the moonshine.

"Close," he answered. "Poughkeepsie."

"Say what?"

"It's a city. In New York. It's where I'm from."

"Well hell, boy! It all makes sense now. You ain't done no living if you're from—-wherever the hell it was you said you come from. I'm here to show you some of the good life you've been missing out on!"

"Let's do it," Dalton said, not quite showing the enthusiasm that his colleague exhibited.

Pike's Peak was located near the edge of the county, and when Harlan pulled his truck into the lot, it was nearly full. Mostly rusted old cars and pick-ups, but a few were newer models that seemed polished to perfection. The pride of ownership was evident on those.

Loud music was blaring from inside. Country Western. "Is that a live band?" he asked as they walked towards the entrance.

"Sure enough. Always got live music on Friday and Saturday nights. No cover charge either."

The place was packed. For a county of less than thirty thousand people, Dalton was impressed at the crowd this club seemed to draw.

"Is it like this every weekend?" he asked as they snaked through the crowd in search of an empty bar stool or table.

"Naw. But this is the first of the month, you know? Payday for lots of peeps around here."

"Oh, got it."

"Yeah, two for one night I'll bet."

Dalton cocked a brow, "Two for one?"

Harlan laughed, shaking his head. "You need to learn the lingo, dude. Two for one is for every dollar's worth of food stamps you get two dollar's worth of cash. Great deal, yeah?"

"Yeah. Can't beat it," Dalton remarked as they finally found a couple of free stools at the bar. Within a couple of minutes, a woman with bleached pink hair slapped a couple of cocktail napkins down on the bar and gave Harlan a glare. She had a ring, pierced through her nose, and Dalton noticed her nails were painted black and were long enough to be talons.

"You got a tab to pay before you get shit to drink, Harlan," she snapped.

Harlan greeted her with a good-natured grin, "Hell, Courtney, I always get shit to drink here whether I'm running a tab or not! Whatcha talking about there, girl?"

"Ha ha," she deadpanned, "Pay up. Sixty-three dollars plus tip."

"Cool your tits," he answered, pulling his wad of cash from the pocket of his Wrangler jeans. Her eyes widened perceptibly and Dalton wondered just how prudent it was for Harlan to be flashing a wad of cash in a place like this, or even in a town like this for that matter. He slapped some twenties down on the bar. "Now set me and my buddy up with some moonshine Jell-O shots, hear?"

Courtney counted the money out, and stuck a couple of bills down her bra. Apparently she lived on the tips. "Now my tits are cooled," she replied, turning her back to them.

Poverty was rampant. There was no light or heavy industry here. Farming was sporadic it seemed. Probably because more often than not, the government had taken to offering farmers more money not to farm than what they'd make if they did.

Welfare, meth labs, and homegrown pot seemed to generate the spending money as far as Dalton could tell.

Courtney placed the Jell-O shots down on the bar, and immediately Harlan handed one to Dalton.

"Two more shots, Courtney. Bottoms up, dude."

Harlan downed his, chewing on the gelatinous blob a bit before swallowing. "Wahooooo!" he bellowed. "Just the way I love my moonshine."

Dalton was less enthusiastic after swallowing his, his eyes watered and he coughed a couple of times. "Man, now that's some potent shit," he rasped, wiping the back of his hand across his mouth. "Hells bells, Harlan!"

"Right?" Harlan replied, laughing. "Don't worry, the more you do them, the easier they go down."

Dalton did a second shot, and found that Harlan was right. Much easier.

"Hey," Dalton said, nudging Harlan, "What happens if we get trashed and Duel calls us?"

"Ain't gonna happen. Too soon. You should know that by now."

Dalton shrugged. "There's no set schedule. Be just our luck something like that would happen. Seems like every time I take one step forward, I get kicked back two. Most money I've ever made. I just don't want to fuck it up."

"You worry too much, buddy. Besides, Duel's not available on Friday nights in the summer and fall anyways. He's at the competition."

"Oh yeah? What's he do? Racecars? Demolition Derby?"

Harlan chuckled, calling out for Courtney to bring each of them a draft beer. "Naw. Duel and my old man are enjoying one of their side gigs along with Duel's boys—you've met them right? Brant and Grant? It's kinda a family tradition I reckon. It's not bad money and they kinda pride themselves on being the best. He's over in Flatwoods, Kentucky with his roosters. Cock fighting. He's got some of the best, you know?"

Dalton shook his head. "No, didn't know. I've seen his boys at the ranch, mostly in passing. They aren't real friendly or open - at least with me yet. I didn't know they raised roosters on top of everything else. So there's real money in that?"

"Hell yeah there is," Harlan replied, "Wanna drive on over and watch? It's a damn circus when they put them spurs on their feet watching them flap and attack the others. Hell, you'll see rooster heads flying as fast as the feathers do!"

Dalton gazed over at Harlan. "Seriously, dude?"

"Swear to fuck it's a good time. And I sure as hell will put my money on Daddy and Duel's birds."

"No. Don't think so," Dalton replied, taking a sip of his beer. "Doesn't appeal to me."

"Oh, what's the matter? They don't dig cock fighting there in Persnickity, New York?" Harlan asked, his voice dripped sarcasm.

"Hey, listen you cocky motherfucker," Dalton said, grabbing Harlan and playfully putting him into a head lock, "I'm just not wanting to get myself in a position of being somewhere that might get raided, you know? Call me paranoid."

"Okay, okay," Harlan gasped, "Let me go you pussy."

Dalton released Harlan and watched in amusement as he rubbed his head. "Jesus, Dalt," he said taking a swig of beer. "You have to admit that's kinda funny. What the hell do you think is in that fucking cargo the Cessna brings in, huh? Bubble gum?"

"Hey man, that's different. It's just us. It's remote. And it all goes down relatively quiet and definitely unnoticed. I don't know what the cargo is and I don't care to know. I was told it was special feed for the miniature horses that hasn't been approved by the FDA or some shit so that's all I need to know."

Harlan scoffed, a big wide grin crossed his face. "Whatever gets you through the night, I reckon."

Harlan considered Dalton for a moment. The guy was quiet and kind of serious most of the time. Good-looking dude with his dark hair and eyes, but something about his demeanor seemed mysterious. He seemed like he belonged in a bigger city. A better, more sophisticated place than Briarton. Beneath his quiet demeanor, Dalton Edwards seemed to be a fish out of water. Somebody who could carve out a real career anyplace they chose.

"What are you hiding from?" Harlan asked quietly. "I can always tell when someone is hiding out and you definitely are running from something."

Dalton sighed, taking another long draw of his beer. "I'm not hiding from anyone. I just have some outstanding warrants in New York and I've got no desire to get in a situation where that becomes obvious, okay? It's why I keep a low profile. But I can trust you, right?"

"Sure, sure you can, dude. Hey—-we've all been there," Harlan replied, smacking him on the back. "Not to worry. I get it. But why'd you end up here?"

"Had an opportunity that fell through. So, I was just hanging out, trying to figure out Plan B when I saw the job posting at the diner. I needed some means of income, so here I am. Grateful as hell, but I can't stay forever. I'm trying to get enough cash saved up to leave the country."

"For real?"

"Yep."

"Canada or Mexico?"

"I haven't decided," Dalton admitted. "They're both options, both easy enough to get into, but I'm thinking I'd make more money in Mexico. Maybe enough to even leave there and head to Cuba."

"Why Cuba?" Harlan asked seemingly puzzled at that choice of a destination for someone like Dalton.

"Dude—are you serious? Hell, what with our prez making nice to them and dissolving all of the embargo bullshit, I figure the tourist business will start booming there. Get in on the ground floor of that, you know? I'm twenty-seven years old, and I want to make my fortune so I can retire at forty."

"Guess I never thought about it, but makes sense. So, you going legit once you're there?"

"Well, I don't know about *that*," Dalton said with a laugh. "I'm more of opting for what makes me the most cash. So, if I can do it legit, I will. If I can't, well then I'm open to other possibilities."

Harlan nodded. "I get that. I'm only twenty-two, so I reckon I have time to figure out my path in life. Not sure I want to stay around these parts forever."

Dalton spoke up, "Hey, what's the deal with Brant McCoy? Does he have an ex-wife around causing him problems? He was all bent out of shape the other day about some fucking bitch that was keeping his kid from him or something like that."

Harlan laughed, shaking his head as he polished off the rest of his beer. "That'd be my sister, Tammy, dude. She made the mistake of getting hooked up with him when she was just fifteen. She thought it was true love. She always thinks it's true love. She's getting ready to pop out another kid."

"His?" Dalton asked immediately.

"Oh, who the hell knows? Might be. Might not be. They can't seem to leave one another alone for any long period of time. It's up, it's down; it's on, it's off. For now, she's claiming it's not his. She's got another dude she's in love with. I reckon time will tell."

"Well, does this drama put a wedge between your dad and Duel? Or you? I mean he's your livelihood at the moment, right?"

"You're only partly right on that," Harlan replied. "You see, Dalton, down in these parts most families have known one another for generations. It's only natural families get in spats. You put it behind you. My daddy went to school with Duel. They were lifelong friends. Now they just kinda tolerate one another in their joint interests. They've had their differences over the years as most families do around here. But you go on, because one hand kinda washes the other if you catch my drift. I'm gonna tell you one thing you didn't know. That hidden landing strip on the mountain you're familiar with?"

"Yeah," Dalton replied. "What about it?"

"Duel McCoy leases the land it's on from my daddy. I've got some job security on that one."

Dalton was thoughtful for a moment. "I don't get it. Why doesn't your dad just sell it to the McCoys?"

"They don't want to buy it. They prefer leasing I guess. Hell, they pay Daddy five grand a month to lease it. It's only sixteen acres and not good for much anyways being up top that mini mountain and all. The old man was gonna timber it but Duel said he'd lease it instead and to keep the trees right where they were. He cleared just enough for that landing strip on the flat part. You still think they're bringing in horse feed, Dalton?"

"Still," Dalton remarked, "it doesn't make sense with all the land the McCoys own down here. Surely they could find another place to put a landing strip."

Harlan laughed again. "You sure don't know much about Briar County, do you? We may be in the sticks, but we're no way in hell off the radar. You'll learn in time. There are reasons for what we do. There are reasons for division of power. And there are reasons one hand washes the other. And there's reasons for minimizing risk."

"I suppose," Dalton replied, draining the last of his beer. "But it sure seems weird, dude."

Harlan laughed and gave Dalton a hearty slap on the back. "You know, you're alright. Getting out for a couple of drinks is a good thing, I reckon. I wasn't sure about you there for awhile, but I gotta say, you're A-okay, dude."

ANDREA SMITH

Chapter 7

Dalton awoke with a splitting headache the next morning. Damn Harlan and his rotgut moonshine he thought to himself as he crawled out of bed and went to the bathroom sink.

He splashed cold water on his face, and rubbed the sleep out of his eyes. That shit had kicked his ass, but he was glad he'd gone. Harlan was a wealth of information once he got liquored up good.

Dalton brushed his teeth and then wandered over to the complimentary coffeemaker that sat atop the small refrigerator in his motel room.

He opened a coffee packet, emptied it into the basket and then took the pitcher of water he always kept there and filled the cylinder. He flipped the switch and waited.

Before the coffee had time to brew he heard his personal cell phone ring from the dresser drawer where he'd been keeping it. He hadn't realized it was already ten o'clock as he pulled the drawer open and grabbed the phone.

"Edwards," he answered, knowing who it was at the other end.

"Let's do brunch," the voice said. "Usual place in Ashland. See you at elevenish."

Call ended.

It was his contact. Jack Reynard. They'd only met twice before in person. The first time, Jack had reamed Dalton for not having shit to report. The second time was better.

Dalton pulled out a clean pair of jeans and tee shirt, dressing quickly, then looked around for his boots. They were on the other side of the bed, so he quickly donned them, grabbed his keys and was out the door before the coffee finished filling the glass pot.

∞

Dalton made it to Ashland by a little after eleven. He saw the dark blue Impala parked in a spot and he pulled his truck into a spot around on the other side of the restaurant.

Jack liked to meet at Jerry's Restaurant because for whatever reason, he loved their food. Dalton thought it was just okay, but it was a good place to meet without drawing attention.

Once inside, he spotted Jack in a booth over in the corner. The place wasn't packed, which would make it a bit easier for them to converse. He took a seat across from his boss.

His real boss.

"I ordered you coffee," Jack said, "You look like hell."

Dalton ran a hand through his still sleep-tousled hair. "Well, shit. Like I had time to primp and still get here on time," he said, managing a slight grin. "Got my first and hopefully last taste of the local moonshine last night."

Jack's lips formed a grim line, and Dalton knew he had concerns about this entire assignment.

"Don't worry, I know my limit."

"So, what's new?"

"One delivery since we last talked. Still not sure who's muling for them on the ground. We're instructed to leave the vicinity before the occupants get close enough to see. Hell, they could be black, white, male, female - got no idea."

"You need to get closer, Dalton. You need to see exactly what's coming in and who they're passing it off to so we can finally get a handle on this."

"Don't you think I know that, Jack?" he growled.

They both grew silent as the server set their coffee on the table and took their orders. Once she was out of earshot, Dalton continued. "These things take time. Trust has to be earned, and I have to make sure I don't draw attention by rushing it."

"That's where it's tricky," Jack replied, pouring sugar into his coffee. "We don't have the time we thought we had."

"What do you mean?"

"Manny found out that one of the local yokels is on the take. There could be more, but for sure they've verified one dirty cop in that county. He's bankrolled by Vince Hatfield. So far, he's not linked to the cartel, at least as far as our agent can tell. So, the dirty cop is protecting Hatfield from something."

"What? The cock-fighting?" Dalton asked, snickering.

"What?"

"Yeah, just found out last night. Vince and Duel have a cock-fighting gig going on. Apparently, there's some good money in it. They hold competitions, so there's probably a pretty good-size ring of them in the area."

"Well, good money to them, isn't chicken shit to the cartel if there *is* a link. Pardon the pun."

"And there's something else," Dalton continued. "The property where the landing strip is located isn't owned by Duel McCoy. He leases it from Vince Hatfield. Aside from that and the cock fighting, it doesn't appear the two families are business partners on the cargo coming in. I get the feeling the two families don't trust one another. Or maybe their individual interests conflict with one another."

"Meaning what?" Jack asked impatiently.

Dalton was thoughtful. "It's almost like a civilized feud if that's even possible. Other than leasing out the land, and the cock-fighting bit, Vince has a full-time job. The family has an obvious passion for demolition cars, but they don't by any means live an extravagant lifestyle."

"Define their lifestyle," Jack commented taking a sip of coffee.

Dalton shrugged, "Mobile homes with additions built on sections, some barns and garages. It appears to be a compound of close-knit family members. But again, I've not had an opportunity to explore the place without drawing undue attention. I need to get closer to Harlan if I want access. Is somebody nervous about the Hatfields?"

Jack shook his head slowly. "Not exactly the family per se. Manny says the chatter he's picking up is related to what's behind this cop who's being paid off. After that shit went down three years ago with the AG and BCI finding the cache of marijuana plants, and then running his mouth linking it to the Mexican cartel in national news, well, things are still sensitive in the area."

"No shit. For the record, I've seen no Hispanics on the ground in the time I've been there. Can't even get close enough to that Cessna to see who's piloting it. Can't see who picks up the cargo, and where it goes. If the attorney general had done what he promised he was going to do back then, my ass wouldn't be living in dog patch, and my gut wouldn't be burning from moonshine right now."

Jack leaned forward, and lowered his voice although nobody was within fifty feet of them. "Listen, you need to find out what the hell Hatfield's got going on that he needs to have a cop in his pocket. And finding it out sooner rather than later would be good. I'm not comfortable with this bit of news. Ingratiate your ass with whomever you need to, but I need something soon so my agency is not left in the dark, got it?"

"I'm on it, Jack. No worries. But if time is now the biggest factor, I say let's pop them on the next delivery. We know that plane is holding something other than weed. I'm betting a shitload of heroin, maybe coke. But my money's on heroin. Hell, the whole state is considered Ground Zero for opiates. How many more people have to die as a result of this shit coming into the heartland?"

Jack was just as frustrated as Dalton with the intricate networking that had taken hold of Appalachia and turned it into an opiate wasteland.

"You know why. For every puddle jumper carrying a load of the latest poison of choice to Briar County, there are a hundred others doing the same damn thing one state over. We have to get the distribution infrastructure in our sights. And that means people, Dalton. Joe Blow at the gas station down the road, Aunt Tillie at the donut shop in town. People have knowledge; they just might not know exactly what it means."

"Yeah, I get that, Jack. Hell, nobody has to preach to this choir. I know that nearly a half-million pounds of this shit came into the country last year. But maybe this farm-to-arm supply chain needs to be dismantled one small piece at a time, have they considered that?"

"Listen, Dalton, we don't set DEA procedure or protocol, we do what we've been instructed to do. And right now, Briar County is the entry point for all of Southeast and Southwest Ohio. My BCI agent is posted in Dayton, and the hub there seems to be the epicenter. We're close. But we can't let whatever else is going on in this particular county fuck everything up. If we bag the couriers, we get nothing. This network doesn't move in a vertical line, there are nodes and redundancies involved. Why take a low-level courier or two, when I want to annihilate the whole fucking supply chain?"

"I don't know about that, Jack. I'll do my best but these people are tight knit. And my gut tells me that maybe it's a one-man show."

Jack grunted, and Dalton knew he was totally passionate about this mission. As well he should be. Jack had lost his son to a heroin overdose. It was up close and personal with him.

Dalton, on the other hand, just wanted to put the bad guys away and shut our borders to the international drug smugglers coming up through Mexico. Small Cessna's like the one that landed the other night could fly virtually undetected using VFR (Visual Flight Rules) and no flight plans had to be filed with the ATC. Their flight paths could be damn near anywhere within the hundreds of miles of porous border that separated the two countries.

Their food arrived and they ate in silence for a few minutes. Finally, Dalton broke the silence. "I've got an idea. I'll see if it works. I'll hit Harlan up to get a feel for whatever other work I can get being that he believes I'm trying to get out of the country. He did say that preparing the landing strip was only part of how he earns his living. The rest comes from the family business I'm presuming."

"Well that's rather obvious, isn't it Dalton? Unless you think legit stuff like demolition derbies or growing tomatoes does the rest," Jack replied tersely.

"Chill, Jack. Let me dig harder to find out what his other source of income is, and how it plays into what Duel has going on. If they've got a side business going, which seems likely, it has to be on their property. Vince Hatfield owns over seventy acres just in Sunfish Township. If he's got a local in his pocket, I need to find out why."

Jack looked up at Dalton. "Have you scoured their property?"

"Yeah, I mean as much as possible from a distance. There's a big metal fab building about three hundred yards behind their barn."

"So, you've been in there yet?" Jack asked impatiently.

"Negative on that. You can only access it from the road that runs parallel to the road they live on unless you're actually inside the gates of their property.

The gravel road behind it looks like an easement between property lines probably made to access pastures with farm equipment. And it's gated as well, so I seriously doubt if that building is for cock fighting. I'll snoop around. The problem is the whole area is like a compound. Several mobile homes spread out around it in a half circle. Kind of difficult to get in and out without notice."

"Well shit, Edwards! That could be the whole enchilada. He could be cutting the heroin with whatever the additive of choice is and making synthetic fentanyl in that damn building."

"But what if the cargo isn't heroin, Jack? What if it's cocaine?"

"Doesn't matter what the fuck the cargo is, Edwards. These asshats are putting homemade fentanyl in any drug of choice. Pretty soon weed will be sprinkled with that shit!"

Dalton felt Jack was overacting just a bit. But he understood why. "Look Jack, at this point, we're still guessing what the hell they're unloading. And the fact remains Vince and Duel are not friends. They're more like business associates who don't particularly like or trust one another. Like at all. No, if something's big going on, those two are not in it together. It's separate."

Jack was thoughtful for a moment, and finally let out a frustrated sigh. "Do you think Hatfield is cooking meth? Hydroponic weed? Maybe they both know what the other is doing and are frenemies for that reason."

"Could be. He's going through a shitload of propane. I've seen that truck there twice in one month on my way into town. It's not even that cold out now. Doesn't really explain why Vince has a cop in his pocket either, but seriously, Jack," Dalton continued with a chuckle, "Did you actually use the word frenemies?"

"Fuck off," he growled, trying not to crack a grin. "I have a sixteen-year-old daughter. I learn from her. But check it out, and let's talk again next Saturday. And in the mean time, see what you can do to get some motion activated surveillance up on the ridge."

"You got it, Jack. Same place, same time?" Dalton asked.

"Yep. Your turn to buy next week," Jack replied, pulling out his wallet. "See you then."

Chapter 8

It was pitch black outside. Dalton was on foot, a pocket flashlight he couldn't use just yet in his backpack, along with his night vision goggles that he couldn't use yet either. For now, he was being guided only by the half-moon and the sprinkling of stars that provided a bit of light whenever the patches of cloud cover moved out of the way.

Once he made his way up the steep, wooded hill, and then hiked down into the ravine, he could use the night goggles to make his way back up to the crest where the land flattened out for a few acres for the landing strip. That time couldn't come soon enough as far as Dalton was concerned.

An outdoorsman he'd never been. Not even a boy scout on his past resume. But he'd hiked up here enough times to know the lay of the land fairly well.

Once he reached the area, he put on his goggles and paced off the yardage he'd calculated he'd need to have the infrared camera activated by the motion sensors installed.

He hoisted himself up the tree that was just on the other side of the landing strip, and with the dark brown Velcro strips he'd ordered, the video equipment certainly wouldn't be visible to anyone around, night or day.

Once he'd secured that camera, he made the trek to the other end of the field to install its twin to another tree. The Cessna had come in from both directions the times he'd been there so this would hopefully lend itself to capturing the plane's tail number for tracking. He also hoped it might provide clear pictures of the couriers that made the drop-offs.

Once finished, he cleared out before some idle hunter or an early morning fisherman crossed his path. It was a secluded area, but not a ghost town by any means.

∞

The following morning Dalton awoke to a loud pounding on the door of his motel room. "Jesus," he growled, looking over at the clock. It was only a little after six. Who the hell would be pounding on his door this damn early?

"Hang on," he yelled, grabbing his discarded jeans from the chair next to the bed and pulling them on. He stubbed his toe on the way to the door, and a soft curse escaped. He jerked the door open, prepared to lay into Harlan if it was indeed him disturbing his sleep on one of his days off.

It wasn't Harlan Hatfield he came face to face with. It was Elroy Driscoll of all people.

"I'm sorry to bother you this early Dalton, but I came here to thank you."

"Thank me?" Dalton asked, rubbing his chin stubble in confusion, "For what?"

"May I come in for a second?" Elroy asked, leaning on his cane. "It won't take but a minute, and it'd be better if we're not seen by some nosey 'Lookie Lou' who might drive by this place."

Dalton held the door wide allowing the older man access to his motel room, closing the door behind him.

Elroy looked over at Dalton. "I know it was you who left that envelope full of cash inside my truck a few weeks back. Twenty-five hundred dollars to be exact. Enough to pay off my delinquency and make next month's payment to Virginia

McCoy, which I've done. Thanks to you, I'll be able to survive until I can get back to work. Ida got an evening job at the nursing home, so we'll be fine until then."

"Why do you think it was me?" Dalton asked.

Elroy gave him a grateful smile. "Because around these parts you never know who's gonna sneak up to my garage, break the lock and steal me blind. My tools of the trade are my livelihood, least they will be again once I'm healed up. I installed a motion-activated spy cam inside the electrical box on the front of my garage last year."

Dalton hadn't considered somebody who lived as simply as the Driscoll's lived would have the need for hidden surveillance. But then again, Dalton underestimated the desperation of poverty that existed in the rural community of Briarton.

"May I ask you why?" Elroy broke the momentarily silence between them.

Dalton shrugged. "I just thought it was a shitty thing to do to somebody down on their luck through no fault of their own I guess."

"Well, son, I will pay you back. It will take some time, but I am a man of my word. Seems to me this county needs more people like you and less people like the McCoys. Their land contract dealings are designed to fail for poor suckers like me and Ida. They feed off of people with their thirteen percent loans, late penalties, and evictions of families who've paid faithfully for months, even years, that have unexpected circumstances pop up beyond their control. I won't forget what you've done for us."

Elroy extended his arm out to Dalton for a strong handshake. "Can we keep this between us?" Dalton asked, shaking Elroy's hand.

"You've got no worries there, son. I know the McCoys wouldn't look favorably on you bailing us out. But please, if there's ever something I can do for you, you will give me a holler, right?"

"Absolutely, Elroy. There's a good chance I'll do just that."

Dalton knew he'd made a trusted ally with Elroy Driscoll. And with the garage's close proximity to the East Fork Ranch during his days off, that just might come in handy at some point.

∞

"Hey Vince, what's up?" Dalton called out as he jumped out of his truck he'd parked at the end of the gravel drive leading up to the compound.

He had spotted Vince Hatfield out in the yard, his head under the hood of one of the two dozen cars he had on the front part of his property.

Kind of an eyesore to passersby, but there weren't any county codes prohibiting it. Dalton figured it was a smokescreen for whatever it was Vince really had going on his land. And precisely in the metal building on the back of his property.

Vince eyed him a bit suspiciously. Dalton had never come to his property before. He knew Dalton and Harlan hung out occasionally, and he'd cautioned his son about getting too thick with a stranger in the community too quickly.

But his son thought he was an expert in dissecting a person's psyche within minutes after meeting them. His boy had a lot to learn.

"Just changing the oil here. What can I do for you, Dalton? Harlan's not around at the moment."

Dalton walked the few paces to where Vince stood watching him. "I was hoping maybe I could do something for you, Vince."

"Yeah? I'm listening."

"Look," Dalton started, shoving his hands into the pockets of his jeans, "I probably need to let you know that I've done things in my past that well, make it necessary for me to start a new life. And being here has been the freshest start I've had like . . . ever. The people here have been good to me. I've been working for Duel McCoy out at the ranch, three days a week, but the truth is; I could use some extra cash. I'm thinking about settling here for good. Tired of drifting."

Vince remained silent.

"Okay, so I guess what I was wondering was whether there's anything else I could do for you to earn more money. I notice these cars here. I'm pretty handy myself. If you need me to work on them, detail them out, whatever, I'm here. Hell, to be honest, I'd like more work just to keep me busy and outta trouble."

Vince took his ball cap off and ran a hand through his collar-length brown hair. "These cars are kind of a hobby, Dalton. I enjoy the tinkering. Don't have plans to sell them off right away."

"Oh," Dalton mumbled, the disappointment evident. "Well, just thought I'd ask is all. I get it. No problem." He turned to walk away, but stopped when he heard Vince's voice call after him.

"Now wait a minute. Let me give it some thought. Harlan seems to think you're an alright guy. I'm picking up hours at my job in Portsmouth now that spring is coming. Might have some odd jobs needing done. Harlan's been tied up with some family stuff. Depends on how picky you are."

"Lay it on me."

"Well, weekends are when I could use some help since I'm going to be working Saturdays for the next month or two. Sunday is our day of rest and going to church. My old lady is stubborn on that. I could use you to come down in the mornings, feed the chickens, and clean out the coop. Then up yonder, I've got a pasture with a few goats. You could feed and water them, rake up the mess in the field, and sweep out the small barn I've got there. I could pay you fifty bucks a day. You up for it?"

Dalton smiled, "I'm in. Start Saturday?"

"Sounds good. I'll have Harlan show you the ropes. Be here at seven, how's that? You should be done by noon so it won't fuck up your entire day."

"Works fine for me," Dalton replied, "Thanks, Vince."

"Oh, and Dalton?" Vince called after him. Dalton turned and looked over at him. "Please keep this weekend gig between us. Duel McCoy might not like you working for me. We don't always see eye to eye on things."

"Got it."

Dalton called Jack Reynard later that evening to push out their Saturday breakfast meeting to a late lunch.

WHERE THE CRAWFISH SWIM

59

Chapter 9

Dalton arrived at the restaurant in Ashland a few minutes before Jack. He went ahead and ordered sweet tea for the both of them. He nearly finished his by the time Jack arrived, looking tired and flustered as well.

"Almost thought you were going to be a no-show," Dalton said as Jack slid into the booth opposite him.

"Had to take a call before I left. Manny called. A couple of the Dayton operatives got busted up in Lorain last night at the regional airport. The courier had swallowed fourteen heroin pellets, and one had ruptured inside of his intestine. He was foaming at the mouth, so his handler calls down to Mexico to find out what to do," he said, shaking his head, "Know what the boss said? Told him to cut the courier open and retrieve the remaining drugs."

The server arrived at their table to take their food order. "Just a salad," for me, Dalton said, his appetite having waned at Jack's news. Jack ordered and once the server was out of earshot, he continued.

"So, Manny's listening to this conversation. And there was nothing he could do without blowing his cover," Jack continued.

"So what happened?" Dalton asked.

"You don't want to know," Jack said. "What do you have for me?"

Dalton handed over the flash drive he'd taken from both cameras early this morning. There'd been another delivery last night.

"I haven't had time to check these out," he told Jack. "Hope they captured something you can use. Plane came in early this morning around one. I had to sneak back before dawn to get these."

Jack put the flash drives in his pocket and nodded. "Anything else?"

"Yeah, got a second job on weekends feeding the animals and cleaning up their shit at the Hatfield place. Started this morning with Harlan showing me the ropes. I was there when he got another propane order delivered. Six hundred bucks. Vince paid the delivery guy in cash. No account. Cash on the barrel."

"Have you been able to get inside yet?" Jack asked.

"Negative. Steel doors always locked. The windows on the building are barred and covered from the inside. There's an overhead door at the far end. The building is fully plumbed. Oh, and get this, he's got two gas driven generators out back of it. No huge electric bills to draw attention to his activities no doubt. Along with that, he's got a couple mini-split 15 Seer heat pumps attached to the steel barn."

"Surveillance cameras?"

"Surprisingly, no. Not on that particular building. Not unless they're well hidden in the trees around the place. But, I think I've got something. They're allowed to burn trash in the county. Vince's got a huge burn pile up in the pasture, behind the goat barn. There's a stack of flattened out corrugated paper he hasn't burned yet. I checked them out. Boxes for flexible tubing, air filters, and grow bulbs. I doubt if he's cooking meth. Probably what we suspected all along, some kind of a grow house for a hydroponic weed operation going on inside that building. It has to be."

"Interesting. You think it's part of the cartel's business?"

Dalton shook his head. "Nah, they're into much bigger bucks. Plus, the fact you said the cartel is curious as to why Vince has a cop in his pocket confirms it. Tells me that Vince is going solo on this operation."

"I agree," Jack commented as the server placed his food on the table and left the check. "That's probably a good thing for now. Don't need the locals getting involved with a pot bust when we've got bigger fish to fry."

"No shit. I'll keep my eyes out. I've got to find out what the rub is between the Hatfields and McCoys. But I'm curious, why don't the local authorities know we're working this? Don't you trust any of them?"

"Not right now. There's been too much of a shake-up over the past year. Some of the deputies are, shall we say, less than stellar? Sheriff is fairly new. I think he's trying to clean up the department, but until we know for a fact that he has, it's too risky right now to clue them in."

Dalton nodded. "Well, keep me posted if Manny gets anything at his end. I'll do the same from my end."

ANDREA SMITH

Chapter 10

Billy Ray Jensen had seen the two black SUV's again in the early morning hours as he went out to his barn to tend to one of his goats that was getting ready to calf.

In the dark quietness of the night, he'd heard a vehicle approaching and when he looked out towards the road, he saw them passing by going towards the highway. This was just too strange he decided. Why didn't he ever see those same vehicles around town during the daytime?

They were always either coming or going from the direction of the Hatfield land. That in itself was cause for concern. The Hatfields were well-known in the county and had been for as long as Billy Ray could remember.

The community whispered amongst themselves about how Vince supported himself and his extended family. He didn't live a lavish life, but still, he had all those cars he tinkered with that appeared to be a hobby. With him being the only source of income, people wondered just how he was able to support everyone at the compound and invest so much money into a hobby that didn't seem to have much of a return.

Billy Ray had heard talk about him being involved with area cock fighting, but that combined with Vince's job surely couldn't bring the kind of money to support his entire family, including grown kids, their significant others and even nephews and grandkids who lived there.

If Billy Ray had to guess, he'd say Vince Hatfield was selling drugs for a living. And it bothered him that the local authorities seemed to turn a blind eye to that sort of thing here in the county where he'd been born and raised.

He made a mental note to nose around a bit. His property bordered Hatfield's, and through his hunting and fishing, Billy Ray knew every trail and path to access the back of Hatfield's land. It was time somebody found out what was going on.

∞

Dalton Edwards had his ear buds in, singing along with the Marshall Tucker Band while he raked the straw up in one of the empty horse stalls. Eight of the miniatures were in the horse trailer behind Duel's pick-up on their way to Lexington, Kentucky to see the vet down there.

"I ain't never been with a woman long enough for my boots to get old. We've been together so long they both need re-soled. If I ever settle down, you'd be my kind, and it's a good time for me to head—-"

"Nice song," a voice behind Dalton said, startling him enough that he dropped the rake and whirled around to see who had crept up on him like that.

"Jesus Christ, Grant, don't be sneakin' up on a body like that!"

Grant was leaning against a stack of baled straw, chewing on a toothpick and grinning like a fool. "Sorry, Dalton, but hey man, you've got a great voice there. Makes me wonder why you're here and not somewhere like, oh say . . . Nashville?"

"Right," Dalton replied, picking up the rake, "I'll keep that in mind."

"What're you doing here today anyway? Friday isn't your day to work."

"Somebody called off. Duel called me early this morning and asked me to fill in since he had to make a trip to Lexington."

"Figures," Grant scoffed. "Wiley Willy. About as dependable as snow in July. I saw the trailer's gone. Daddy must be off to the vet."

"Yep," Dalton answered, continuing to rake. "That's what he said. Are the ponies sick or something?"

"Falabella Miniatures, Dalton. Not ponies, *Falabella Miniatures*. There's a difference."

Dalton stopped and rested his chin against the handle of the rake. "Excuse me, Grant. I stand corrected. Are the *Falabella Miniatures* sick or something?"

Grant shook his head. "Nope, just a check-up with their vet in Lexington. They are delicate creatures to some extent. Daddy wants to make sure they stay good and healthy."

"Seems like Lexington is a long haul for a check-up with a vet. No local veterinarian around to do that?"

"Wouldn't trust these locals to look after a pet rat. Daddy insists on using the finest of equine veterinarians. And Lexington has the best. So, how do you like it here in hillbilly country, Dalton? Seems like a strange place for anybody to settle unless they didn't have to, you know?"

Dalton shrugged and resumed raking. "One place is as good as another," he replied. "It just depends on your outlook I guess. I kinda like these parts. People are nice. The countryside is beautiful, and I can stay on the down low."

"And that's important to you?"

"It is. I have my reasons."

"Anything around here capture your interest so far?" Grant asked, studying Dalton as he continued raking.

Dalton wasn't sure what Grant was getting at with the last question, but he needed to react as if it was totally innocuous. "Well, I think I'd like to try out the fishing down here. Used to fish a lot up around Lake Erie when I was a kid."

"That so?"

"Yep. Any recommendations on the best spots for fishing?"

Grant was thoughtful for a moment. "There's a pay lake in Sunfish. Loaded with trout and Large Mouth Bass. If you're looking to bank fish, Briar Lake is your best bet. Bass and Bluegill, and if you're lucky you might even catch some Northern Pike since the Scioto River feeds into it."

"Sounds just what I'm looking for. Isn't that just down the road from Hatfield's place?"

"It is," Grant replied. "This time of year, dusk is the best time to go out. Some folks night fish, but those would be the die-hards."

"Thanks for the info, Grant. I better get back to it unless there's something specific you needed me to do?"

"Nope. Just checking on things in the barns. Make sure the stalls all have fresh straw. The horses are a bit jumpy after a trip to the vet. Daddy sometimes has to give them some medication so they rest."

"Got it," Dalton replied.

"Good luck with your fishing, dude."

After he left, Dalton was pretty damn sure Grant had been on a fishing expedition of his own.

Chapter 11

"That all ya need, Dalton?" Ella Johnson asked sweetly as she bagged up his bait and hooks, and placed it in the crate with the rest of the fishing gear he'd purchased from Johnson's Fish and Tackle, the local store for fisherman in the county.

"I think that'll do it, Ella," Dalton answered pulling out a wad of bills to pay.

"How you likin' our little town so far?" she asked, placing the bills in their proper slots in the register drawer, and counting out his change.

"I like it fine, Ma'am," Dalton replied.

"It's a shame you're not seeing anyone around here. I think you'd make a great catch for one of the local gals. Hey, we have a church social the fourth Saturday each month. It's from seven to eleven at the First Unity Church on Wilson Street. Now the hall is right behind the church, can't miss it. Why don't you come?"

Ella Johnson was the sweet, plump, motherly type. He'd seen her around town a few times. Dalton knew she meant well, but he wasn't about to get roped in to a "fix up" that would further complicate his life and his mission.

"I'm really not on the market for a gal right now, Ella." The words were out of his mouth before he gave it more than two seconds thought.

Did he really say that? Dalton Edwards, the semi manwhore, not interested in chicks? He'd had his share of one-nighters, and even a couple short-term relationships. He never thought he'd say those words let alone think them. But that was how it had to be until he figured what the hell was going on in this county. He didn't need a sexual liaison clouding his thoughts or judgments. The secrets lay deep; and the people were closed-mouth with each other it seemed. He was still a newcomer. He didn't need complications.

Her eyes widened a bit, and she blushed.

"Oh, oh . . . I'm sorry—I mean, I understand. I sure didn't mean to be so pushy with you Dalton. My lord, sometimes I'm just too much of a busy-body for my own good. I hope you don't think I'm prying into your personal life. Nothing worse than a nosey busy-body, right?"

Her plump face had turned beet red as she stumbled over her words. She was totally flustered and Dalton was puzzled by her obvious embarrassment over the conversation.

He smiled at her, "Ella, it's fine, really. It's no big deal. I think it's nice of you to look after folks around here, especially new members of the community. No need to apologize, okay?"

Her head bobbed up and down in agreement. "You come back and see me again, okay? I promise I won't be trying to fix you up again."

As Dalton headed towards the door of the store to depart, he heard Ella call after him, "Good luck on your fishing, Dalton! Hope you land a whopper!"

∞

It was dusk when Dalton tossed his line out into the water of Briar Lake. He hadn't lied when he told Grant he had fished as a kid. His family would always make a summer trek to the shores of Lake Erie and rent a cottage. Boating, fishing off a pier, and swimming were all part of his summers back then.

He liked the quiet tranquility of the spot he'd chosen to set up his folding chair. It was surrounded by budding trees, leafy foliage with the occasional squirrel skirting up a tree trunk and disappearing into his nest.

He placed his ear buds in, listening to Tim McGraw. It was funny how he'd taken a real shine to country western music since he'd been here. Most every store, restaurant, laundromat, and radio station played nothing but country western, but it was a pleasant deflection from the music he used to listen to before his assignment to Briar County. It was laid back, the lyrics were distinguishable. And the message was always clear.

He'd had his pole in the water for about an hour with no bites. It was getting dark out and Dalton was about to reel in his line and call it an evening when he heard the sound of footsteps coming down the slope, the sound of boots crunching the leaves from last fall on the ground were unmistakable. He pulled his flashlight from the pocket of his jacket and twisted around to shed light on whoever was approaching.

It was a man looking to be in his late fifties. He had a folding chair, tackle box, and pole slung over his shoulder. He was wearing a fishing jacket with an assortment of bobbers and hooks dangling from it. Definitely a seasoned fisherman, Dalton thought.

"Hey there," the guy called out, "are they biting?"

"Not for me," Dalton replied with a laugh. "But it's probably me, not the fish. Kinda rusty I guess."

The man dropped his pole and gear, and offered his hand for a shake. "Didn't mean to infringe on you there, buddy. This is my usual spot too. I'm Billy Ray Jensen, live up the road a piece. Haven't see you around, but then I don't get off my place much now that I'm retired from the outside world so to speak."

Dalton shook hands with the guy. "Glad to meet you Billy Ray, I'm Dalton Edwards, and yes, fairly new to the area and totally ignorant to successful fishing around here it seems. Haven't fished for years and usually fished from a boat or pier."

"Let me have a look at your lure and bait, son. Maybe I can give you some tips on what works for me."

Dalton reeled his line in and Billy Ray grabbed the bobber, and studied the bait still untouched on the hook.

"Well hells bells, boy," he said, bursting into a rumbling laugh, "What are you fishing for, a plastic fish? You can't use plastic worms to catch anything here," he continued laughing, but it was a friendly laugh; not mean or condescending.

"Ella recommended it for bass fishing. That's what I was hoping to catch."

"Ella Johnson can't tell a fart from a turd," he said snickering. "In early spring, the best thing to use to hook the bass who are staging for the spawn is to use a lipless crank bait lure, a bigger hook than what you've got here and some fresh crawdads as bait. Here, watch me," he instructed as he attached the lure, hook, and bait to his own pole.

With the snap of his wrist, he cast his line out into the dark water, and within several minutes, got the first tug on his line. He jerked it once, and then reeled in what looked like a largemouth bass.

"Got me a five pounder with this one," Billy Ray said, unhooking the fish and tossing it into his pail. "Now you see, Dalton, that's how it's done."

And for the next hour, Dalton and Billy Ray Jensen fished and chewed the fat. Billy Ray was a talker, no doubt about that. Dalton learned he was a widower, retired from the sheriff's department of an adjoining county, and was drop dead sure the Hatfields were selling some sort of illegal contraband from their compound.

"You know Dalton, I fish a lot. Generally, night fishing on account of I have a farm to tend to during the day. Nothing big, mind you, a few goats, some chickens, and sheep. Keeps me busy, supplements my retirement income. I harvest hay in the fall for some of the horse farms in the area. Other than that, my recreation is fishing and hunting. Done it all my life. Lived here all of my life, and I can tell you one thing, stuff has changed around these parts—and not for the good."

"Is that right? I've only been here for a few months. I kinda like it around here."

"What is it you do for a living? I'm guessing it's not supplying fresh caught fish for the restaurants or grocery deli," he said with a chuckle.

"I work part-time over at the McCoy East Fork Ranch. And then odd job here and there. I like the pace of Briarton. The people seem friendly and all."

"Virginia McCoy is one of my customers for baled hay. A saint that woman is. Done so much for the community. Even has some non-profit benevolent organizations she runs. Seventy-five years old and still going strong. Give her a lot of credit. Now her grandsons? They might be a different story."

Dalton chuckled. "I've met them, mostly in passing cause they work the barns the days I'm off. I mostly interact with Duel. But I did happen to see his younger boy, Brant, come around one day totally out of sorts. Something about his kid and the kid's mother?" Dalton replied, hoping for more information on that situation.

Billy Ray didn't need a formal invitation to share his views on that topic.

"Why in the hell that boy got mixed up with the likes of Tammy Hatfield is beyond me," Billy Ray started, shaking his head.

"First off, the girl was like fifteen years old! Wearing her jeans so tight you could see her religion! No surprise there when she got knocked up. But I can tell you this; it didn't sit well with Brant's family. Especially with Brant living out there with her in one of those trailers. I mean, c'mon, what girl at sixteen even knows what love is?"

Dalton shrugged his shoulders in response. He knew Billy Ray had more to share.

"Brant, on the other hand, should've known better. Now I hear she's kicked him to the curb and has some other guy living there and is due to have another baby in a matter of weeks. Custody battle going on now that Tammy is knocked up again. It'll be interesting to see who the daddy is on that one being her trailer seems to have a revolving door - know what I mean?"

Dalton chuckled and nodded affirmatively. "How did Brant's family take him fathering a child with a minor?" Dalton asked. "Were they pissed off?"

Billy Ray thought for a moment. "No, I really don't think so. It was Duel and Sally Jo's only grandbaby, and Virginia's only great-grandchild. From what I know, the little girl - let me think . . . yeah, her name is Madison - they call her 'Maddie', she spends a lot of time out at the ranch which is a good thing," he said, nodding. "It's a much better environment than at the Hatfield place."

"What's your take on the Hatfields?" Dalton asked, leaning back in his chair. The guy liked to talk. He wasn't going to waste this opportunity to gather info he might not already know.

Billy Ray gave a snort, and then continued on, "The Hatfields have an almost cult-like existence. All these adult kids or other relatives living there with their spouses or significant others. Don't see how they're making ends meet which is why I'm convinced, regardless of Vince's job, there's money coming in from the side, know what I mean?"

"Well," Dalton replied, "I don't know Vince all that well. He's kinda quiet, but he did give me some odd jobs on the weekend, so that much I appreciate. I've partied a couple of times with Harlan. Seems like an okay dude."

Billy Ray turned to him. The glow from the lantern he'd brought clearly reflected his surprise at what Dalton had just told him. "Boy," he said slowly, "you need to watch yourself being tied up with them. One thing I can tell you is that something has been going on in the last six months or so up around his place. You know he has that huge metal building, right? Can't figure out what he does with it. I can tell you this though, there's been a few times I've been out night fishing late, and by that I mean early hours of the morning. On my way back to my truck, I've seen two black Suburbans coming down the road from his land. Thing is, I've never seen them around during the daytime. I figure he's growing weed up there. Can't prove it. Decided to just keep out of it. Never know where danger lies. You be careful, you hear?"

"Thanks, Billy Ray. I've seen the metal building but never been in there. My job is just cleaning the barns, feeding the chickens and goats, and cleaning up after them."

"Well," Billy Ray replied, "My property borders his towards the back. I've been tempted to snoop around myself."

Dalton was uncomfortable with that. All he needed was an ex-cop getting tangled up in something he knew nothing about. It would likely make his mission unnecessarily complicated.

"It seems to me that the local authorities might already be privy to this, don't you think Billy? I mean, how would the black SUVs tie into the Hatfields?"

"Yeah one would think, but I've not seen any action on their part, you know? The only reason I've tied them to Hatfield is because they come from that side road that borders their property. Only two landowners bordering this here road. Me and them. And I know for a fact it ain't me," he said with a chuckle.

"Yeah, but Billy, it's not a dead end road, ya know? I mean it goes on for several miles doesn't it? Could be coming from lots of other places other than the Hatfield place, couldn't it?"

Billy ray shrugged, "A road to nowhere basically. Yeah, I mean it eventually leads into the nature preserve, but seems like a stupid way to get from there to here on a road full of ruts and big rocks when there's better routes to take from that area."

"Well," Dalton continued, "I don't pretend to know a lot about how law enforcement works down here, but sometimes don't they work off the grid until they get concrete evidence of something going on?"

"That's how it's supposed to work in a perfect world, but in case you haven't figured it out yet, Briar County ain't a perfect world."

Dalton shrugged. "Still, you never know what might be going on. Tell you what, if I see anything screwy, I'll let you know in case they are turning a blind eye to it for one reason or another. I know you're a law abiding man who one can trust, at least that's how I see it."

He gave Dalton a nod. "I think you're probably a good guy too, Dalton. If you come upon anything, you can trust me with it. After all, my career was in law enforcement. I have connections in other counties. Briar County law enforcement, well, I don't trust 'em, just saying. Pretty bad history of corruption."

"I'll do it for sure, Billy. No worries."

"You might as well take them with you, Billy. My motel room doesn't have a kitchen."

"Why you staying there at the motel, Dalton?" he asked.

"Didn't think I'd be staying this long. Was headed further south. Might be looking for a place to rent. Feel like I belong here."

"Yeah," Billy Ray said, "I think maybe you just might. Tell you what, you take those fish up to Stella at the diner. Have her clean and fry these up for you. Tell her to fry it in some apple butter with a squeeze of lemon juice. You'll love it, I swear."

"Thanks, Billy," Dalton replied, reaching out to shake his hand again. "It's been real nice fishing with you, hope to see you again."

That night when Dalton returned to his motel room, he had three Largemouth bass in his cooler thanks to Billy Ray Jensen.

∞

Dalton had just crawled into bed after his evening fishing excursion when his private cell vibrated on the nightstand. Hell, Jack never called this late, he thought as he grabbed it up and hit the screen to accept.

"Yeah," Dalton said.

"Tomorrow. Let's meet at Sally's Diner just down the street from Jerry's.."

End call.

WHERE THE CRAWFISH SWIM

Chapter 12

"Just a sweet tea for me, darlin'," Dalton said flopping down in the booth across from Jack. "Whew, I'm pooped," he continued, "Don't think I've ever worked as hard physically as I have been since being down here."

"No doubt," Jack said, "Maybe you need to exercise more brain less brawn."

Dalton cocked a brow. "So, what? You telling me I'm moving too slow? You never did give me any feedback on the surveillance video. I need some feedback here to know what my next steps are, Jack."

"Because we didn't get shit off the video. Two guys on the plane wearing hoodies so their faces are overshadowed, your boss Duel, and a tail number that's fake."

"Fake?" Dalton asked, his brow furrowing. "How the hell can the carrier get away with that? Aren't those tail numbers recorded when the plane lands at airports or refuels somewhere along the way?"

"Typically, yes. But what if this particular plane doesn't need to refuel from Point A to Point B and back to Point A?"

Dalton nodded. "A private mule. Network couriers. This has to be bigger than I thought. It's not coke or meth. It's got to be heroin."

"No surprise there being the whole fucking state is Ground Zero for this shit," Jack replied.

"I know, I know. I've heard it before, Jack. No need for reminders. I got it."

They remained silent as the server placed the sweet tea in front of Dalton, and refilled Jack's coffee.

Jack poured some cream into his coffee and stirred it thoughtfully. "What else do you have?"

"There's a retired law enforcement local living down the road from the Hatfields. Does a lot of night fishing. He's seen the ground mules a couple of times now. Black SUV's headed to Highway 32, one goes east, the other goes west. What we don't need is him getting involved at this point."

Jack nodded. "So work faster, Edwards. If we can't get the boys in the air, we'll need to get the boys on the ground. Gotta give something to the AG what with the elections coming up in a few months."

"Yeah, it's always politics first, isn't it?"

"Welcome to the world of the D.E.A., Dalton."

WHERE THE CRAWFISH SWIM

Chapter 13

Dalton was just starting his Sunday chores at the Hatfield place when Harlan came out to the small barn that housed the chicken coops where he was busy filling the feeders and trying his best to avoid getting pecked.

He turned to see that Harlan was wearing a suit that didn't quite fit, looking totally uncomfortable, one hand tugging at his striped tie that seemed to be choking him.

"Wow," Dalton said with a laugh, "Look at you. Never have seen you that dressed up for Sunday services, Harlan. Trying to impress somebody special?" He tossed him a wink.

Harlan looked flustered and definitely not in the mood for levity it appeared. "Funny, dude," he said, "Naw, it's a baptism service today. Tammy is finally getting around to baptizing her and Brant's kid. Big doings afterward. Daddy wanted me to come out and pay you since you'll be finished by the time we get back. Harlan reached into the rear pocket of his suit pants pulling out a wad of bills from his wallet.

"For yesterday and today. Daddy says to make sure you put the padlock on the front gate when you leave," Harlan said, his arm reaching back to replace his wallet. It missed his pocket and landed in a pile of straw Dalton hadn't spread yet. "Shit," he said, bending down in an attempt to retrieve his wallet and everything that had spilled out of it.

The sound of material ripping, caused Harlan to straighten up immediately, his right hand quickly reaching behind him to assess the damage of the too tight dress pants.

"Fuck," he growled, "I knew I'd put a little weight on, but not that much! Dammit!"

"Here," Dalton interceded, "Allow me to help out here." Dalton squatted down, slipping the contents back into the wallet and brushing some of the straw out of the way.

He stood and handed the wallet over to Harlan. "Turn around and let me see how much damage you did to your fancy drawers there, Harlan."

Harlan's face turned a shade of red as he grabbed his wallet and backed up toward the door of the barn. "S'okay, dude, I got it," he said with obvious awkwardness. "Got to go change, I'm already running late. Later, Dalton."

Harlan exited the barn so fast, Dalton had to chuckle. He'd left like his ass was on fire. As soon as he was sure Harlan was well out of sight, he squatted back down and brushed the straw back from an item he hadn't returned to Harlan's wallet. He picked up the electronic key card, wiping pieces of straw from it.

It was an RFID smart card. There was no commercial printing on it, which told Dalton it was used to get access to one of the buildings on the Hatfield land. He slipped it into the pocket of his jeans, knowing what he needed to do once he'd finished up his chores.

∞

Back in his motel room, Dalton went to the closet and grabbed his briefcase off the shelf and placed it on the bed. He input the combination, and when the lid flipped open, he grabbed the small RFID NFC card reader and plugged it into the USB port on his laptop.

Pulling up the software, he placed Harlan's key card on the reader and waited for the code to upload to his computer. He then placed a blank card onto the reader, hit "clone" on the device, and within seconds, he heard the verification beep that the code had been replicated on his card.

"Easy peasy," he said aloud. "Now we've got to get Harlan's card back to him." No problem there. Monday was one of Dalton's days off. He'd hit up Harlan early with some excuse for doing so.

ANDREA SMITH

Chapter 14

The sun had barely risen when Dalton started up his truck and headed down the road toward the Hatfield place. He knew that Vince had already hit the road for his first shift job in Portsmouth, so the gate would be unlocked.

They had several security cameras around the property, but he had no issue with getting Harlan's ass out of bed before he had a chance of discovering he'd been missing something from his wallet.

He pulled his truck around the drive toward the last mobile home on the left. He got out, took the few steps up to the porch and banged his fist on the door of the trailer. From inside, he could hear Harlan cussing, his voice still heavy from sleep or a hangover.

"Hold on, I'm coming, no need to break my fucking door down!" Harlan yelled as he flipped the locks on the door, jerking it open. "What the hell?" he said, his eyes squinting up at the sunlight filtering in through the open door.

"Mornin," Dalton called out cheerfully. "You ready?"

Harlan had no choice but to step back when Dalton's frame closed in on him from the open door.

"Ready for what? What the fuck are you talking about?" Harlan scratched his jaw in confusion.

"Dude," Dalton said, "Remember we talked about it last week? At the bar? You mentioned going four-wheeling and we agreed on Monday since I don't work on Mondays."

Lines of confusion still lingered on Harlan's face. "Seriously, dude? Shit, I must've been pretty damn drunk. It ain't ringing no kind of bell for me."

Dalton released a disappointed sigh. "Remember you telling me about racing four-wheelers over on the ridge?"

Harlan was thoughtful. "Yeah, yeah—I remember that part, I just didn't know we actually made plans to do it, is all. Hell, I've got shit to do around here today, Dalton. Being tied up all day yesterday and last evening put me behind on stuff I need to get done here. Hang on, let me go get my jeans on. Do me a solid, will ya, and get some coffee going on the machine over there? Coffee's in the cupboard above it."

"Sure thing," Dalton said, turning towards the kitchen area while Harlan, clad in boxers and a wife-beater, disappeared toward the back of the trailer to get dressed.

Dalton saw Harlan's keys and wallet on the countertop that divided the kitchen from the living room. He quickly dug the key card from his pocket, slipping it inside the wallet before he continued on to where the coffeemaker sat and started preparing the brew.

Harlan returned a couple of minutes later, wearing jeans and pulling a sweatshirt over his head. He ran a hand threw his tousled hair, pulled a couple of mugs out of the cupboard, and remained silent until he'd filled them with the freshly brewed coffee. "Cream or sugar?" he asked Dalton.

"Nope, black is fine, thanks."

They sipped their coffee in silence. It was unusual for Harlan to be as quiet as he was this morning. Dalton figured either he wasn't a morning person, or he was wracking his brain trying to remember a conversation they'd never had.

"So, listen Dalton," Harlan finally spoke, breaking the silence between them, "We'll need to take a rain check on the four-wheelin' today. I've got a list of chores to do before Daddy gets off his shift or he'll have my hide."

Dalton shrugged. "No problem, buddy. Anything you need my help with? I've got the whole damn day at my disposal. Be glad to lend a hand to a friend."

Harlan looked over at him. "We are friends, aren't we?"

Dalton smiled, "I'd like to think so."

Harlan shifted a bit. "Well then, uh . . . now don't take this the wrong way or anything, but that's all we are, Dalton. Just friends, know what I mean?"

A puzzled look planted itself on Dalton's face. What the hell was Harlan getting at exactly? He was clueless, until Harlan finished his thought.

"I mean, I don't judge people, believe me. I believe everybody should live and let live, no matter what their preferences are. It's just . . . well, it's just that I don't swing that way, brother."

"Dude," Dalton said, still clueless, "I'm not following you. You need to just spill whatever it is that's on your mind here."

"My sister talked to Ella Johnson's daughter-in-law the other night and Ella had told her that you're . . . well . . . you're gay?"

And then it dawned on Dalton. It was all he could do to contain his laughter. Ella Johnson had obviously mistaken the response he'd given about not being in the market for a gal as meaning he was gay.

That explained Harlan's uneasiness the day before in the barn when he'd ripped the ass end out of his pants; and the way he was in a hurry to cover his boxer clad frame just this morning when Dalton had shown up unexpectedly.

Dalton belted out a laugh that rattled the windows of Harlan's trailer. "For Chrissake, Harlan," he guffawed, "You know me better than that! I was just trying to avoid having her fix me up with God knows how many available women from her church. I didn't tell her I was gay, I just told her I wasn't in the market for a chick. Jesus! She sure as hell twisted that around, didn't she?"

Harlan appeared a bit skeptical momentarily. "Well, I mean, you haven't seemed interested in checking out any of the chicks around here, so it kinda made sense and all . . . you know, that you might be queer," his voice trailed off.

Dalton stood up, still chuckling, "As soon as I find one that meets my fancy, and isn't already taken, don't worry, I'll make my signature moves," he replied with a wink.

Harlan didn't look totally convinced. If Dalton had learned anything at all since living in these parts, he knew for a fact it wasn't a community known for embracing diversity. Like at all.

"Besides that Harlan, if I was queer, trust me, you wouldn't be my type," Dalton said, giving Harlan a hearty slap on the back. "So, do you need my help today or what?"

"No, thanks on the help," Harlan replied, grinning, and then flipped him the bird, "And fuck you on the not being your type comment."

Dalton got up to leave, but Harlan called after him just before he hit the door. "Meet you at The Peak for a beer later?"

"Sure thing," Dalton replied.

"I'll be up there around eight. See ya then mother fucker."

Dalton left knowing that Harlan was none the wiser on anything, and that was a good thing. Things were brewing, and although Dalton couldn't put his finger on the particulars of it, his instincts were now in high gear and he sensed shit was about to get real.

Chapter 15

Dalton had made sure he hadn't had more than two drinks when he'd met Harlan at 'the Peak' that evening. He also made sure he'd bought Harlan a good share of moonshine Jell-O shots to get him good and loaded.

He kept the conversation low key, mentioning only that it'd been a while since they'd been called out to the landing strip, and wondering if something was going on with Duel's little side gig.

"Fuck that landing strip," Harlan scoffed, "We don't need no landing strip. Got bigger plans," he said, his voice now slurring.

Dalton wasn't sure what Harlan meant by bigger plans, but when he pressed Harlan for the deets, his friend clammed up.

It was one a.m. and the bar was empty as Courtney helped Dalton get Harlan into his truck after he'd scarfed his keys earlier. "Don't worry Courtney," Dalton assured her, "I'll pick my truck up in the morning."

"No worries, Dalton. Hope he doesn't puke all over you," she said with a laugh as she went back inside the bar to close up.

Dalton's plan had been executed perfectly so far. He only hoped Harlan was passed out for a while as he needed the cover of being in Harlan's truck to unlock the padlock on the front gate for access to the property. The Hatfields always locked the gate after dark.

Jack had been on his ass so hard, he knew he shouldn't wait, hoping for a better opportunity when nobody would be around the family compound, which wasn't often. But tonight they were all tucked in, lights out.

Dalton located the key for the padlock on Harlan's chain and extricated it without having to turn off the truck. He didn't want Harlan waking up just yet. He quickly got out of the truck and unlocked the gate, jumping back into the truck and driving it towards Harlan's trailer.

He parked Harlan's truck on the far side of his mobile home so that he could slip out and make tracks towards the metal building just a few yards behind the burn barrels.

He exited the truck quietly, deciding Harlan could sleep it off in his truck. He wasn't about to wake him up and drag him inside the trailer. Time was of the utmost importance.

He'd dressed in black exactly for this purpose, and like a ninja on steroids, Dalton made quick and silent tracks to the back of the property.

Once he arrived there, he glanced around the area for any surveillance apparatus.

Thankfully, there were no motion activated lights on the building which told Dalton they didn't want to draw any particular attention to this building. It was so far back from the main cluster of the individual dwellings, he doubted anyone still up would have seen the lights anyway.

Once he reached the main door, he swiped the cloned smart card down the pad and breathed a sigh of relief when the red light turned green and the sound of the lock mechanism clicking. He turned the handle and stepped inside of the building, pulling the heavy metal door shut behind him.

Inside the building, grow lights with timer switches illuminated the interior. There were several rows of steel tables that held marijuana plants, in various stages of the growth cycle.

Clip-on fans were posted throughout the building to circulate air, and Dalton glanced upward to see a sprinkler system most likely timed to dispense mist to keep the humidity at the optimum level for the cannabis.

This was a hydroponic weed operation. With all the gauges and timed environmental conditions implemented, it was clear Vince and Harlan were skilled in the business.

Dalton counted about sixty-five plants. Certainly not a major grow operation, which was puzzling since there was plenty of room for more plants.

He quickly did the math in his head and figured the total harvest value at around $200K. It didn't make sense they weren't harvesting more to get a better return on their investment with the operation. There certainly was more than enough room.

Dalton tripped over an extension cord that was stretched across one of the aisles and skidded to the floor, landing on his ass. Luckily his boot had drug one of those heavy-duty rubber industrial mats that had been placed on the floor of the building along with him so his ass had landed on the thick cushioned rubber instead of the hard concrete.

Had he not tripped, he might have missed that as he got to his feet, dusting off his backside and bending over to pull the mat back into place, he noticed what it had been covering.

A trap door. On a concrete floor? But that's exactly what it was. Great care had to have been taken in the construction of this metal fab building, which by all appearances had a partial basement that had been cleverly hidden.

Dalton certainly was not prepared for what he was about to discover as he descended the wooden steps to the underbelly of the Hatfields' grow operation.

WHERE THE CRAWFISH SWIM

Chapter 16

It was two days before Dalton could get a meeting with Jack. Harlan had cussed Dalton out the following day when he'd ran into him at the gas station on his way to work at the McCoy place.

"Nice leaving me out in my damn truck, Dalton. Everybody loves waking up in their own puke."

"Sorry, dude," Dalton had replied as he filled up his truck, "Don't you remember me trying to get your ass out of the truck and you telling me to leave you the fuck alone?"

Harlan had ran a hand through his hair, his brow furrowing as if trying to remember something that clearly hadn't happened. Dalton should have felt like a shithead, but it was all about the greater good.

"Naw, can't say that I do," Harlan replied, "Guess I'll have to take your word on that one. Took me all damn day to clean out my truck, not to mention the splitting headache I couldn't get rid of."

Dalton had put the gas nozzle back onto the pump, screwing the cap on his tank. "Well, I'm sorry dude. Thought you could handle your liquor better than that. I had to hoof it back to the motel. It was no picnic for me either. Next time we'll have to put you on a two shot limit."

"Fuck you, Dalton," Harlan had replied, "I can drink your pansy ass under the table any day of the week." He had said it with a big grin so Dalton had known he was forgiven.

∞

"So, what have you got for me, Edwards, that you couldn't have sent it over the cloud?" Jack asked, his voice not hiding his irritation that Dalton had scheduled this meeting mid-week, which happened to interrupt his vacation.

Dalton pulled out a flash drive with the pictures he'd taken of the Hatfield grow operation, and the more interesting operation he'd discovered inside the hidden basement of the metal building. He handed it over to Jack.

"I didn't want to send this via the cloud because of security reasons obviously. I'm not sure exactly what all this means, but here are the actual pics I took with my burner phone," Dalton said, pulling up the photos he'd saved in an album he had titled 'Crossfire Hurricane.'

"Catchy title," Jack replied dryly, "Where have I heard that before?"

"Nowhere good," Dalton replied with a wicked laugh.

"So, what the fuck am I looking at?" Jack asked, flipping through the photos. "It's obviously a grow operation, not a huge one at that. What the hell is Hatfield doing?"

"Hydroponic poppies. You know Jack, the poppies that produce the nectar that led to two opium wars back in the mid-nineteenth century?"

"Shit, Edwards. I know what harvesting poppies yields, but what the hell? Hydroponically grown? How large is this grow room? What's the opium yield per plant? How long does it take from seed to harvest? And what is Hatfield doing with it? Chemically producing heroin, morphine, codeine?"

Dalton took a sip of his coffee, patiently waiting for Jack to chill a bit. He knew dropping this bomb of sorts would promote a lot of questions and complicate the purpose of their discussion.

"If you'll quit with the string of questions, I'll give you my perspective on what's going on with the poppies, Jack."

Jack shifted in his seat and gave him a nod, taking another gulp of his coffee.

"Okay, so Vince, he's got over four hundred poppy plants down there, and they look close to harvest. I took a bulb from one of them," Dalton said, reaching into the pocket of his jacket and placing the bulb on the top of the table.

"Is he making heroin down there?" Jack asked.

"Nope," Dalton replied, "There's no lab equipment or additional chemicals required for that. My guess is Vince and Harlan are doing one of two things with this."

"I'm listening."

"The easiest process would be if they're extracting the sap in its milky form, and combining it with the harvested weed to make Black Russian Hash."

"Street value?" Jack asked.

Dalton shrugged, doing the math in his head. "Providing their grow operation is in lock-step with the opium yield, probably a half million."

"Your second scenario," Jack prodded.

"The hydroponic weed is separate from the poppies. There is absolutely no indication at that site that the Hatfields are doing anything other than harvesting the opium sap as a raw material. Meaning they're letting the sap ooze out, allowing it to darken and then scraping the gum into balls or bricks, wrapping them and selling them to a refinery. Low tech. Easily moved to a processor who'll handle the chemical enhancements necessary to produce a number of end products."

Dalton might've been a screw-up within the DEA because of his extracurricular activities that ultimately had landed him smack dab in the middle of Appalachia, but he had earned his degree in Forensic Science. He knew his stuff.

"What are the end product options, Edwards? Feels like I'm having to pull teeth here," Jack grumbled.

"Black Tar Heroin, Morphine, White Heroin, about any type of street opioid you can think of. Then, of course, if the processor has several gigs going, it could be mixed with crack, coke, meth for speedballs, and of course, synthetic fentanyl. My gut tells me, *that* is what's going on here. Vince has low risk, can move it domestically, and combined with his weed grow he can cop more than a million bucks a year without much out of pocket cost."

"So," Jack said, leaning forward and poking the poppy bulb with his spoon, "You think he's doing this shit independently of the shit coming in on that landing strip?"

"Absolutely," Dalton replied, chewing on a toothpick. "And I think it's a fairly new endeavor for him. There's more tension between the two families. And get this: we haven't had a shipment come in for a couple of weeks now. I tried to get some info out of Harlan, but all he told me was that they had bigger plans. Might just be that Vince pulled the plug on allowing Duel to lease his land for that landing strip."

"Shit. This is heating up. You need more agents down here?"

"For what?" Dalton asked, "I've been here for months. This whole county is a tough nut to crack. More agents coming in under cover would do nothing to expedite this investigation. In fact, it would more than likely cause panic. You don't seem to get how this community operates. Like nothing I've seen before, even when I lived in Texas."

"The way I see it, Edwards, is that we now officially have two drug operations going in separate directions. One major, and one bush league at the moment, but all that can change in a heartbeat. I'm uneasy about this. Who would have thought this sleepy little county in southern Ohio is potentially a hodge podge of opioid activities?"

"Just give me a little more time, Jack. I really think I'm getting closer. I can't be sure of anything with respect to Duel's activities. If Vince did cut him off, he could very well have another landing place that he's keeping to himself. I just need a little more time watching the back roads so to speak."

"Whatever that means," Jack said with a snort. "This whole thing is turning out to be a twisted ride that so far has led us no closer to busting those at the top of the cartel."

"Jack," Dalton said succinctly, "Has it ever occurred to you that there just might be more to the local dynamics than just the cartel? If in fact there really is a cartel at work here."

"Not following," Jack replied. "Our intelligence indicates the cartel; an offshoot of the Espinoza Cartel, is at play in that area. Do you know something different?"

"All I'm saying is that intelligence isn't always accurate. Sometimes it's cleverly planted for other reasons. I mean have you considered that maybe these people eventually won't need the cartel if in fact they are involved? Think about it. Right now the borders are pretty accessible. Things could change. The politics could change. Who's to say that one or both of these families don't have a Plan B up their sleeves in case that happens? We got a presidential contender that keeps harping about a wall. That sure as hell could put a crimp into all those muling routes that prefer to bypass the points of entry, don't you think? I did my fucking time in McAllen, Texas if you'd take a minute to access my assignments with the agency. As far as I'm concerned, Homeland Security could fill the Rio Grande with gators, copper heads and water moccasins and I wouldn't miss a fucking night's sleep over it. Hell, maybe PETA could even declare the Rio Grande Valley a sanctuary for endangered Western Diamondbacks or something. I can see the slogan now: Bring us your venomous reptiles. No snake will ever be turned away. This might be dog patch, Jack, but these people are nobody's fools," Dalton finished.

Jack gave Dalton a nod. "Feel better Edwards? Ready to get off your soapbox for a minute? You're preaching to the choir here. I know you're frustrated. I know I'm on your ass. I know it's not moving fast enough for the agency. I know you're just one guy stuck in a town that feels like it's right out of Deliverance. But listen to me, and listen good: things have changed. The cartel chatter has all but died on this front, which is why I have been on your ass to give me something—anything goddammit, just bring it!" he hissed.

They both took a moment to calm down. Their conversation had heated up more than it ever had before, and several of the customers were looking over at their table.

Finally Dalton stood up to leave. "The decrease in chatter could mean a couple of things, Jack. I've already pointed that out and I think you know that as well as I do. Trust me when I say it's all coming to a head soon."

"And you know this how?" Jack challenged.

"My gut is telling me that. I don't question my gut, Jack."

And with that Dalton turned and left the restaurant, never knowing that his parting words bore more truth than he had ever intended.

ANDREA SMITH

Chapter 17

It was Friday night. Dalton hadn't seen Harlan since that Tuesday morning at the gas station before he'd gone to work at East Fork.

Duel had called him early Wednesday morning and told him he wouldn't be needed for the rest of the week because his boys were there to help with the breeding and they could handle Dalton's chores as well. He assured Dalton that he could resume his duties the following Tuesday, and to enjoy his time off.

Dalton had found it strange, but then again, this whole area was strange. It seemed as if the cloak of secrecy was drawing itself tighter around the community. He hoped like hell he hadn't in some way cracked his cover.

He decided to do some night fishing and try to get his head wrapped around whatever it was that had been gnawing at his gut all week. Maybe the solitude of fishing in the night air, with nothing but the sounds of crickets and the soft lapping of the water against the rocks would serve to help with that.

The air was crisp, cool and quiet. The night sky was clear, and a blanket of stars, along with the new moon cast their reflective glow on ripples of the water. They hadn't had much rain this spring, but Dalton had no clue whether that would affect his chances of catching anything worth keeping. Hell, he didn't really give a damn.

He put his pole in the water, and attached the handle to the rod holder on his chair so he could light a cigarette. He didn't smoke often, but tonight he felt the need.

He settled back in his chair, taking a long drag on the cigarette and tried to push all of his conflicting thoughts from his head. The truth was he'd come to like Harlan. But he couldn't let that cloud his judgment or influence his ability to dissect the facts as he knew them.

The Hatfields had a grow operation. Not a huge one, but big enough to qualify as a Class 1 Felony. The poppies were a fledging business, yet quite lucrative and under the radar. This had to be Vince and Harlan's first crop, which would explain Harlan's cocky comments and the fact there hadn't been any recent deliveries on the ridge.

Something had changed. There was no way Duel knew about the poppies, and no way the cartel, if they were even involved, cared about the weed grow operation. It was pocket change in comparison to what was coming in on that Cessna. And Duel didn't seem to be overly panicked about the fact there hadn't been any deliveries in nearly four weeks.

Dalton's mind was spinning theories when he heard footsteps behind him.

"How they biting Dalton?" a familiar voice rang out.

Billy Ray Jensen.

Fuck. That was it.

Dalton wasn't sure how he knew it. Maybe it was purely instinct, but Billy Ray Jensen held the key to this recent turn of events. And Dalton needed to find out exactly what Billy Ray might've done to cause the change in the dynamics.

"Hey, Billy Ray. Not biting for me so far, but that should be no surprise, right?" Dalton said chuckling. "Maybe my luck will change now that you're here being a seasoned fisherman and all."

Billy Ray set up his chair and meticulously prepared his fishing line with live bait. Once he'd put his line in the water, Dalton struck up a conversation with the older man. He started with basic stuff: the weather, local gossip, the upcoming opening of a racetrack in Scioto County.

Billy Ray loved to talk, and he was talking up a storm, but not one word about the Hatfields, which Dalton found odd considering their last conversation. So finally, Dalton brought it up.

"By the way, Billy, have you seen those black Suburbans around lately?" Dalton asked, recasting his line.

"Can't say that I have. Did see something odd though a couple of weeks back. One of my goats was getting ready to kid and got out of the gate. I'd gone out to check on her and saw that she was gone. It was pretty late so I got me a flashlight and started walking my property to find her. When I was close to the fence line where that dirt road separates my property from the Hatfields, I heard an argument going on."

"Oh yeah?" Dalton replied, "who was arguing?"

"Sounded like Vince and Harlan. They were standing outside that big metal building of theirs. I shut off my flashlight so they wouldn't see me in case they looked yonder my way. Vince was telling Harlan his mind was made up and wasn't nobody going to change it. Harlan told his Daddy he was being a fool and putting them all at risk. Vince told Harlan to watch his mouth. Said that he made the decisions around here and he preferred to conduct his business with no outside interference."

"What business was he talking about?" Dalton asked.

Billy Ray shrugged, reeling in his line, and disengaging a carp, tossing it back into the river. "Hate those bottom feeders," he said with a laugh. "Oh . . . I was talking about the fish, not the Hatfields. Um . . . well, if I had to guess, it's probably whatever he's got going in that metal building. Have you had a chance to find out?"

"Nope," Dalton answered. "I'm only there about ten hours a week. Saturday and Sunday mornings. It's hard to snoop around much what with all the people living in that complex. But think about it Billy. If those Suburbans haven't been around in a spell, could be they weren't connected with the Hatfields at all."

"Maybe," he said recasting his line into the water, "but I got tired of sitting around trying to put the puzzle pieces together and it was impossible to stop. Couldn't help it. Must be in my blood being that I was in law enforcement all those years. So now, it's someone else's puzzle to solve."

Dalton tensed. "What do you mean?"

"I don't trust the local law enforcement. Been too many officers on the take if you know what I mean. So, I used my own methods. I set up a sweet little motion activated video recorder with a timer. Put it up in a tree in a location that would catch those Suburbans on film. Checked it daily. Finally one morning when I checked, there they were. I turned the digital files over to a trusted acquaintance of mine. Told him I suspected the Hatfields were behind it, and running drugs of some sort. He said he'd look into it."

Fuck.

"Not to be nosey, but I'm assuming you meant somebody in law enforcement? Thought you didn't trust them much?" Dalton asked, since clearly he'd received no communication to the effect that the D.E.A. or B.C.I. had been notified. If Billy

Ray had gone to a local yokel, God only knew what kind of screw up was on the horizon.

"Let me put it this way, Dalton. Trust is earned, not given unquestionably. The person I enlightened is somebody I trust whole-heartedly. All I know is that I haven't seen them again, and my camera is still where it was, so it looks like whatever they were doing here has come to an end."

"Maybe so," Dalton said, a feeling of uneasiness seeping in with Billy Ray's revelation. "How long ago was it you reached out to whomever it was you reached out to Billy?"

Billy squirmed a bit, apparently not willing to share anything further on the specifics with Dalton. He cleared his throat and looked Dalton straight in the eye. "Now listen, son, I'm going to give you some advice. You need to watch your back. Something is likely to go down, but you have to understand that these things take time. I know you've been working over at the Hatfield place on weekends, but is it really worth it? I'd hate to see you get caught in the cross hairs. You might do well to give up your little job there. I see no good coming of it."

"You might be right, Billy," Dalton replied, "I don't see any good coming from it either."

ANDREA SMITH

Chapter 18

Dalton reported for work at the Hatfield place Saturday morning. His senses were now on high alert since Billy Ray had shared what he'd done with Dalton a couple of weeks back while they were fishing. It might explain why there hadn't been any deliveries in over a month - or did it?

There could be other reasons for that, in particular, the argument Vince and Harlan had that Billy overheard. He'd need to fill Jack in on the latest when he met with him later that day.

Everything at the compound seemed normal. Harlan came out to where Dalton was mixing grain, chewing on his signature toothpick. "What's new Dalton?" he asked.

"You tell me Harlan," Dalton replied. "Things seem a bit tense around these parts lately. What's going on?"

Harlan shrugged his shoulders. "Beats me. Plenty around here to keep us all busy. We like sticking together, know what I mean?"

Dalton nodded. "I do."

"Sometimes it's just best to keep close and maintain a low profile if you catch my drift."

Dalton knew Harlan was sending a message. He wasn't sure of the intent. He remained silent filling a bucket with the grain mix to feed the goats.

"Hey, Daddy says once you finish here if you'd stack the bales of straw we just got in over at the small barn against the far wall."

"I'll do it," Dalton replied. "What are you up to today?"

"Aww . . . not much. Hey, Tammy had her baby night before last. A baby boy. She named him Barton. I'm headed to pick her up from the hospital. Her boyfriend finally found himself a job and can't leave work."

"Well tell Tammy congrats for me," Dalton replied. "How does Madison feel about having a baby brother?"

Harlan laughed, "Who knows? At two years old her world is pretty much all about her. See ya later, Dalton."

"Later Harlan."

∞

Jack was already at their meeting place sipping coffee when Dalton slid into the booth across from him. "Just an iced tea for me darlin'," he said as the server approached, "With extra lemon slices on the side."

Jack gave a slight snort. "You sure do fit in well down here, I give you that Edwards," he said. "So what's the word?"

"You tell me," Dalton replied in a hushed tone. "You got my message about the convo I had with a local. Who's looking into shit down here?"

"I've checked with partner agencies," Jack replied, "I don't know who this guy went to, but it wasn't any of the state or federal authorities. This totally blows your whole damn assignment down here, you realize that, don't you? You've been down here for six friggin' months, Dalton, and what have we got? I'll tell you what we've got: We've got some videos of a plane landing with a bogus tail number; we've got unidentifiable people delivering unknown cargo, oh and let's not forget, we've got some hydroponic weed that barely rises to a first degree felony. The most we can nail them on are the poppies growing in the damn basement! So, we are now totally fucked on what the cartel had going. There's been no chatter, there's been no more planes landing, and we have got *nothing*," he hissed.

Dalton had never seen Jack so pissed, but he understood his frustration and anger. Hell, he felt it too. "I know, I know Jack, but what the hell could I have done to prevent Billy Ray Jensen from going to some unknown party he supposedly trusts on pure speculation?"

"Well dammit, the guy was former law enforcement wasn't he?"

"Yeah, yeah," Dalton replied, "But he initially said he didn't trust the law enforcement agencies. Said he'd seen too much and didn't trust many people. At the time it seemed like he really didn't want to get involved."

"Well it looks like he did," Jack snapped. "And it's no damn coincidence that the timing of his involvement coincides with the last delivery of whatever it was that Cessna was bringing in."

Dalton gulped some iced tea. "Then why aren't we privy to whoever it is who's pulling those strings?"

"That's what has me worried the most. He may have gone to local law enforcement, but they'd need probable cause for a search warrant and it seems like that has not happened, yet the shipments have stopped. I don't like this at all Edwards. I hope to hell you haven't fucked this one up."

"What the hell, Jack?" Dalton replied, clearly pissed, "What about the Intel from *your* end, huh? You haven't even *confirmed* which branch of the cartel was involved to my knowledge. They all have different M.O.'s and fuck-off that I might be in your eyes, how in the hell can I properly strategize if I don't know where the chatter is coming from, huh? Is it Jalisco, Sinaloa, Juarez - or maybe we're dealing with the Gambinos or the Geneveses, huh? Fuck it, I did the best I could with what information trickled in so don't give me shit about it not happening fast enough to suit you and the higher ups. This isn't your run of the mill urban wasteland for Chrissake! This is po-dunk nowhere."

"Keep your voice down, Dalton," Jack hissed, "Calm down. We don't need further complications. I'm going to call Manny to see if he has a read on anything changing in the Dayton hub. I'll be back in touch with you tomorrow morning latest. Just keep your eyes and ears open."

"Anything else?" Dalton asked quietly.

"Yeah," Jack said tossing a wad of bills onto the tabletop, "Watch your back and stay safe. I can't guarantee you haven't been made."

WHERE THE CRAWFISH SWIM

Chapter 19

One Week Later . . .

Dalton sat on the bed at his motel room, and took another swig of whiskey. He couldn't shake the scene he'd walked into early this morning.

The blood.

The carnage.

The whole magnitude of having the members and close significant others of one local family shot dead, execution style in the quiet dead of the night of Briar County, Ohio was unfathomable in Dalton's mind.

Especially since it was right under his nose. His watch. He somehow felt responsible at the very least for not seeing it coming; for not sensing the imminent danger, for having no clue how or why it had all gone down. And for not preventing it.

Dalton wasn't sure how or when it happened, but the murder of Harlan Hatfield seemed like the loss of a friend. He knew that sounded fucked up.

Realistically, Harlan was one of the bad guys. One of the guys that he'd been tasked with busting once he'd figured it all out to the point where it would bring the cartel down with them. He wasn't the brains behind the operation, but he'd been a willing participant nonetheless and that was exactly what had precipitated this massacre.

Regardless of all of that, he saw Harlan as being the kind of guy, who in any other circumstance and environment might've just been a dude Dalton would've hung out with, rough edges and all. He'd made Dalton see things in a different way for whatever that was worth.

Actually, when Dalton thought about it, the whole experience of being down in this thinly populated rural county, lost at the foothills of Appalachia, a mere dot on the map for the State of Ohio, had given him a different perspective on life - and on survival. It certainly wasn't a place he'd ever have chosen to live. His first impression upon arriving in the county months ago had been: It could've very well have been the filming location for the 1970's Cult Classic movie, 'Deliverance.'

Over time, he'd managed to lift the county veil of secrecy to some degree, but not nearly enough to have prevented the massacre of one family it seemed.

After he'd been grilled by the local yokels, swarms of law enforcement from bordering counties infiltrated Briarton. Dalton was instructed to stay in town and be available for further questioning.

Back in his motel room, his private cell vibrated in the pocket of his jeans.

Jack.

"I've got several DEA agents on the scene down there. Want to tell me what the hell went down with the Hatfields? Eight people shot execution style? A bundle of cash tossed around one of the bodies, who does that?"

"Got no answer Jack. What's your Intel saying?"

"The fucking AG is running his pie hole along with some BCI spokesperson. They made fast tracks down there that's for damn sure. But as usual, they're going with the Mexican Cartel theme, no *specific* cartel named naturally, as if they all fucking look alike, and a large hydroponic pot grow operation."

"That's bullshit, Jack! What about the shitload of poppies being harvested in that hidden grow lab below?"

"No poppies found there. Not even a petal, Dalton."

Dalton had felt his jaw drop with this bit of news. He rubbed the stubble on his chin desperately trying to put the puzzle pieces together in his head. "How is that possible?" he hissed.

"You tell me, Edwards. It wouldn't be the first time an underpaid agent switched sides."

"Fuck you Jack!" he yelled, "Fuck you for even thinking that, much less saying that to me!"

"Calm down, Dalton. The truth will come out eventually, won't it? In the meantime, you're to sit tight right where you're at. Keep your cover if that is even possible, and let the FBI and BCI do their work. Don't get in their way, do you understand?"

"I wouldn't think of it Jack," Dalton replied pushing the screen to END CALL.

Fuck Jack.

Fuck the D.E.A.

That's when Dalton had opened his bottle of Jim Beam and turned on the television to see the live coverage carried by local news stations. Even the cable news stations all over the country were running a news crawler at the bottom of the screen mentioning the execution-type murders of eight family members in Briar County, Ohio.

He turned to a live report now rolling on a Cincinnati network station. A reporter from that station had a mic held up to one of the Briar County Sheriff's deputies, asking questions about the discovery of the bodies earlier that morning.

"We were getting ready to serve warrants on the compound later that morning when a phone call came in around seven-thirty. A male caller who does occasional work for them discovered two bodies in the main house. Once deputies arrived on the scene, a full search was done on the premises. That's when we discovered six more bodies who had apparently been shot and killed as well."

"Can you identify all of the victims?" the reporter pressed.

"We're not at liberty to disclose the names of the victims until all the next of kin have been notified."

"I understand," the reporter continued, "Any sense of what the motive might have been for this . . . massacre?"

"Again, we have B.C.I., F.B.I., D.E.A. and local authorities working together to thoroughly investigate this case. It would be premature at this time to render any conclusions or toss out theories without allowing the local, state and federal officials time to complete their investigations."

Search warrants?

Dalton grabbed his cell and called Jack Reynard back, pushing aside for the moment that Jack was at the top of his shit list.

"Reynard," he answered, his mood obviously still prickly.

"Jack, a local deputy was just interviewed by a Cincinnati television reporter. He told the reporter the county was preparing to serve warrants on the Hatfield compound."

There was a pause. Then Dalton heard Jack growl from the other end. "Sounds like the dirty cop Vince Hatfield had in his pocket either parted ways, or had a better offer. This is a fucking mess, Edwards. Sit tight. I'll be down in the next couple of days. I don't trust anyone anymore."

Dalton took another shot of whiskey.

He'd drink to that.

Chapter 20

The last few days had been almost like an invasion in the small community of Briarton.

Law enforcement of all flavors was crawling over every nook and cranny in the county. The network and cable media was omnipresent, eager to shove their mics into the faces of the locals to ask questions, get opinions, or urge them to share backgrounds and relationships of the slaughtered victims.

Of course, the spotlight attention on the tight knit community was spawning rumors faster than a melting snow cone in hell.

Dalton had made sure to be out and about, stopping in at Pike's Peak the day before funerals of the six members of the Hatfield family were to take place. He still was officially employed by the D.E.A. He was still technically undercover, and so it was still his responsibility to see if loose lips might provide solid tips.

He was nursing a draft beer at the bar, when Courtney came up, wiping the bar down in front of him. "So there, Dalton, how's it going?" she asked.

He was gnawing on a toothpick, the same way Harlan used to do. Probably a habit he'd picked up along the way. "It's fucked up, Courtney, what can I say?"

"That's a fact," she said nodding. She stopped wiping for a moment to study him. There was a pause, and Dalton knew what was coming next.

"How . . . how bad was it when you went in there?" she asked quietly.

Morbid curiosity. He knew more than one person would ask him about that now that he was out and about with the rest of the community, in mourning for the loss of eight people of their community.

"It was as bad as you could probably imagine," Dalton replied honestly. "Don't think I'll ever be able to totally scrub the images from my mind."

She shook her head. "I can't imagine how horrific that must've been. It sure has people around here rattled good. Why would somebody do this and how could they possibly have gotten away with it?" she asked.

Jimmy Lee Jackson, one of the other part-time workers for the McCoys came up to the bar, standing to the right of Dalton. "Can I have another Bud, Courtney?"

"Sure thing," she said, moving down to the cooler at the end of the bar.

"Heard they're pretty sure it was the Mexican cartel who done them in," Jimmy said to nobody in particular.

Dalton turned to look over at him. "Oh yeah? How do they figure that, Jimmy?"

Courtney popped the cap off the Bud, and placed it on the bar in front of Jimmy who had now lowered his girth down onto the bar stool next to Dalton, slapping a five dollar bill down on the bar. Courtney wasn't making a move to grab the money until she heard what inside information Jimmy apparently possessed.

Jimmy was going to keep everyone in suspense until he'd taken his first long draw of his cold Budweiser. "Heard one of the local cops talking to Duel about it yesterday at the ranch. Said the fact that the killers left all the youngins alive points to cartel policy. Plus the fact they left forty-eight thousand dollars in neat piles around Vince is also the mark of the Mexican cartel."

"How so," Dalton asked, taking a sip of his draft beer. He knew enough about the cartel to know the shit Jimmy was spewing was inaccurate. The cartel didn't care whose blood was shed when it came to retaliation. They'd kill puppies, kittens and yes, even babies and toddlers to prove their point, and to inflict fear so that anyone they dealt with knew exactly what the repercussions would be if ever crossed. There was no code of honor or conduct with those bottom feeders. And they sure as fuck didn't slaughter eight family members over a pot grow operation.

"Duel did the math," Jimmy continued, "The cost of a funeral down here is around six grand apiece. Do the math, six times eight? Forty-eight," he replied giving a nod.

"Wow," Courtney said, finally picking up the five and taking it to the register. "I surely didn't know all that."

Yeah, because it's horseshit Dalton thought to himself. The Mexican cartel foots the funeral bills for those they slaughter? Yeah. Right.

"Why would Duel know the cost of their funerals?" Dalton asked.

Jimmy was taking another swig of his beer. "He was going to start a fund to help with the burial expenses until the cop told him about the money left there at the scene. It ain't rocket surgery," Jimmy said with a laugh.

"Hey, why was the cop talking to Duel about it anyway?" Dalton asked, "Was he trying to see if little Maddie saw or heard anything that night?"

"Naw," Jimmy replied, "It was just a courtesy visit by the cop when he'd heard Duel had wanted to start a burial fund and all. Wanted to let him know there was no need for it. And little Maddie wasn't with her mom that night anyway."

"Oh?" Dalton pressed. "I didn't know that."

"Yeah, she was staying with Grandma Ginny that night. What with Tammy's newborn and all, Maddie's been with the McCoys more than normal. Good thing too. Can you imagine what kind of fucked up that might've caused that kid for the rest of her life had she been there?"

"No shit," Courtney piped up, hanging on every word coming out of Jimmy's mouth. "Hey, I heard Brant is taking this real hard. I think he never stopped loving Tammy if you ask me."

Jimmy nodded. "Yeah, he's a mess, that's for sure. Now he's gonna be raising that little girl without her mama. It's a tragic situation for sure. You goin to the funerals tomorrow Dalton?"

"Yep," Dalton answered, not looking forward to it, but knowing he needed to be there. "Duel gave me a few days off paid because of . . . well, because of what I saw."

"Yeah, man. That must've been some crazy shit. Duel's a righteous man, though. I guess when something like this happens, it shows you who in the community is ready, willing and able to step up to the plate."

"You got that right," Courtney said, "I'm taking off to be at the funeral. Then we're going to open up afterwards. Duel is paying for a memorial reception here for the Hatfields. It's open bar and catered-in food."

"Damn," Dalton remarked, "That's pretty damn generous of him. Didn't think he got on all that well with the Hatfields."

"'Round these parts Dalton, any differences or spats of the past with folks are laid to rest when they are. It's bad Karma to withhold forgiveness or carry on grudges against the dead."

Dalton was thoughtful. "I guess I never saw it that way, but it makes sense."

Chapter 21

Dalton was dressed in a suit that he'd had to buy in Portsmouth for the funeral the following day. He parked his truck in the already over-flowing parking lot of the Dry Creek Church of Christ. Just as he was walking up the steps of the church, trying to loosen his tie a bit due to the warm and humid day, he heard a throat clear behind him.

He turned and saw it was Jack. He was in a dark suit with sunglasses, and merely nodded at him, not attempting to acknowledge him any further than that lest someone question them as being acquainted.

The various local media and cable networks had already set up their cameras. The reporters on assignment were televising live as the rest of the county residents piled into the church. There was also a plethora of lookie-loos from parts unknown who crowded into the standing room only wooden church.

Inside the packed church, Dalton looked around and spotted Courtney already seated in a pew, midway up the aisle, waving for him to join her as she'd apparently saved a place for him to squeeze in next to her.

Dalton seized upon the opportunity and walked up the aisle, taking a seat at the end of the pew as she wiggled over to make more room.

She immediately leaned over and whispered, "Are the hearses out front yet?"

Dalton nodded and whispered his response. "They are. Just pulled up as I was coming in."

Right then, the first chords of organ music began to play. Dalton looked up to the right side of the church, and saw the organist playing was Ella Johnson. As Dalton peered around the rest of the church, he saw the McCoy family seated in a pew near the front of the church, Duel, his wife, both sons and Virginia McCoy who was holding Tammy and Brant's daughter, Madison on her lap.

Across the aisle were seated, what Dalton could only guess were the remaining relatives of the Hatfield family, some cousins who still lived in the area and some older aunts and uncles who, according to Courtney, had come up from Sandy Hook, Kentucky.

They were all dressed in black. Several of the females in the group were already dabbing at their eyes as the organ music played softly and the intermittent sounds of sniffling continued. The wooden floor of the church creaked as the first of the six caskets, placed on the aluminum biers, was being wheeled down the aisle past the congregation.

From above, the choir members in the loft began singing the first verse of Amazing Grace. The congregation stood and faced the aisle as the parade of caskets rolled by them. Dalton swallowed as he saw that each casket bore the name of the occupant on a placard attached to the flower arrangement on top.

Vincent Harlan Hatfield.
Mary Beth (Stevens) Hatfield.
Raymond Earl Hatfield.
Harlan James Hatfield.
Tamara Grace Hatfield.
Darrell Edwin Hatfield.

By the time the caskets were all lined up at the front of the church, the intermittent sobs had turned to near constant wailing.

The preacher took the pulpit and gave the mourners several moments to collect themselves while he motioned for everyone to sit down.

For the next thirty minutes, bible verses and gospel readings were recited by the minister. Dalton could see nearly every member of the community present, and many strangers to the area as well. He could tell those who were there on official law enforcement business from those who were part of the curious media, out to get the whole story.

Dalton looked around and caught a slight wave from someone on the other side of the church. It was Elroy Driscoll. It looked like Elroy was back in good health. Dalton hadn't seen him except in passing since the day he'd come to his motel room to thank him. Dalton gave him a smile and a nod, and continued to peruse the people around him.

He didn't want to be obvious, but so far there was one member of the community Dalton hadn't spotted: Billy Ray Jensen. Of course he knew that there'd been no love lost between Billy Ray and the Hatfields. Despite personal spats of the past, the whole community had pulled together on this one, so it seemed strange to Dalton that the Hatfields' closest neighbor would not have put aside any old grudges or past animosity, in order to pay respects to this massacred family. He wondered when grudges and slights of the past died? What good did it do to allow them to linger on?

His attention was drawn back to the minister's voice as he introduced the person who had asked to deliver the eulogy for the Hatfield family.

He watched as Duel McCoy rose and made his way up the few carpeted steps to the pulpit, adjusting the microphone to accommodate his taller stature.

"Good morning family members, friends, neighbors and visitors who are here today to share in our grieving for the loss of this family. A loss that is both horrific and unheard of in our peaceful community.

"Many of you might wonder why I'm giving this eulogy today. My answer is this, I wanted to. Briar County has been the home of the Hatfields for generations, just as it's been the home for my family for generations.

"Our parents and grandparents farmed and worshipped together; their children played sports and attended school together; and our children did the same. My granddaughter who sits over yonder on my mother's lap has lost her mother. We grieve for her. No child should ever have to grow up not remembering the woman who gave life to him or her; to forget a mother's touch, or a mother's kiss, or the loving comfort a mother provides for her child each and every day of their life. But Madison Hatfield McCoy will surely have to grow up without those very things.

"Vince Hatfield and I played Little League together as kids. We went to the same schools from kindergarten through high school. Heck, we even competed for the same girl a time or two. We had some good times over the years, hunting and fishing together, worshiping in this here House of God, watching our kids grow up.

"Oh, that's not to say we didn't scrap with one another a time or two, but anyone in Briar County can tell you that's just kinda the way of life around these here parts.

"At the end of the day, Vince was a hard-working, God-fearing man, who loved his family and didn't deserve his untimely demise. None of his family or their significant others deserved this horrible and tragic end to their lives. And standing here, before you and before God, I want to say that none of us will rest until justice is brought to those responsible.

"'Vengeance is mine sayeth the Lord.' Well folks, I'm not looking for vengeance mind you, but I am looking for justice. I hope everyone sitting or standing here today remembers that once we leave this church and put our brothers and sisters into their final resting place. There can be no peace of the mind or the soul until we seek and find justice for those responsible for taking the lives of eight people here in Briar County."

∞

Pike's Peak was packed. Dalton knew he couldn't say five times quickly that string of words because of the amount of beer he'd already imbibed.

True to Jimmy's word, Duel McCoy had indeed funded this memorial reception on behalf of the Hatfield family. The way people in the area could eat and drink, Dalton guessed it had set him back a pretty penny.

He'd stayed mostly to himself, trying not to get too tanked because after all, he was still technically on assignment, albeit, he had felt the free-fall from grace days earlier, and Jack's terse conversation at the cemetery that afternoon did little to affirm his future employment with the agency.

After the graveyard services, Jack had walked up next to him as he was leaving the cemetery to head back into town. He had spoken quickly and concisely to Dalton. "Keep a low profile, Edwards, let the experts who are down here do their jobs without interference. Stay put until I give you the word to head back to Columbus."

That was it.

No details; no further meetings between the two of them scheduled. For all intents and purposes, Dalton felt he would go down for a failed mission, which he could handle. What he couldn't handle was the fact that eight people were dead and maybe his failure to crack whatever gang or cartel had been part of the operation, played a major role in that.

Everyone in the community was on edge and for good reason. No matter what type of secrets they held, it was nothing compared to the blatant, dead-of-the-night massacre of eight people in this small town. Eight long time residents of the county; and for now the AG and BCI people were pointing the fingers at some elusive, yet-unnamed Mexican cartel over a big marijuana grow operation which was a bunch of horseshit and they knew it.

"Hey you," Courtney said, coming up to him from behind the bar, "You doing okay, Dalton? Seem awful quiet there. This is supposed to be a celebration of their lives. It's tradition around here after a wake and burial."

Dalton shrugged. "Guess I just can't celebrate murder," he said. "Sorry, I didn't mean it to come off that way, Courtney. It all just doesn't sit well with me. This county seems to be full of law enforcement and investigative experts that don't know shit from shinola."

She giggled. "Shit from Shinola, huh? That's an oldie, how old are you, Dalton? My granny uses that phrase and she's damn near ninety."

Dalton gave her a wry grin. "Yeah, I have one of those too. Probably where I picked it up. I'm twenty-eight. You?"

Courtney gave a huff, and put a hand on her hip tossing him a glare. "You're not ever supposed to ask a lady her age," she chastised gently, "Don't you know anything about women, Dalton?"

"Well, hell, you asked me," Dalton challenged. "Thought those gender rules went by the wayside a long time ago."

She laughed. "Yeah, yeah, I get it. I selectively choose to revert back to them I reckon," she replied. "I'm thirty-four. Today I'm feeling more like sixty-four. Been a long day. Glad I got some help here though. You ready for another?"

"Sure," Dalton replied finishing off his beer, "hit me."

Courtney grabbed a fresh frosted mug from the cooler, and went to draw Dalton another draft.

"You get anything to eat, Dalton?" a voice behind him asked. Dalton turned to see Duel McCoy standing there.

"Hey Duel," he said, holding his hand out for a shake, "Not yet. Don't want to kill the buzz I got going. Have a seat why don't you?"

Duel slid onto the bar stool next to Dalton, and pushed his empty glass, signaling Courtney he was ready for another.

"You doing okay?" Duel asked, "Been kind of quiet sitting here all by your lonesome. Everyone else is back in the banquet room. Lots of food still out."

"Yeah, I plan on going back there in a bit," Dalton replied as Courtney placed his mug of beer down on the bar.

"Bourbon?" she asked Duel.

"Yep, neat."

"Hey Duel," Dalton continued, "I think it's a damn nice thing you've done for the community by hosting this memorial for the Hatfields. I liked your eulogy by the way. Kind of surprised me."

"Oh yeah?" Duel asked, "Why's that?"

Dalton grabbed a toothpick from the shot glass filled with them on the bar, his thoughts of Harlan rampant in his head, and popped it into his mouth. He chewed thoughtfully on it for a moment, choosing his words carefully. "Well, to be honest, I didn't think you and the Hatfields were particularly fond of one another, leastwise as long as I've been around these parts."

Courtney placed Duel's drink in front of him and grabbed the bill he handed her. "Keep the change, Courtney," he said with a smile. He then turned back to Dalton. "It's like I said in church, both families go way back. Generations back as a matter of fact, so it stands to reason over the years yeah, we've had our scraps and disagreements. But I can say this with one hundred percent certainty, if it had been my family who were the victims of this, this... hell, I don't even know what to call it, Vince Hatfield sure as hell would be doing the same thing that I'm doing. Now that's a fact, son."

He took a swig of his bourbon, then pushed off the bar stool, and gave Dalton a firm pat on the back. "Get something to eat, Dalton. I'll see you at the ranch on Wednesday."

And with that, Duel McCoy disappeared back into the crowd of people milling about near the banquet room.

∞

Dalton wasn't sure what time it was when he felt somebody smack his head with . . . . something.

"Locking up Dalton. It's time to wake up so this girl can close up, go home and get some sleep. C'mon, get up. Hit the head or whatever you need to do while I count the register." Courtney's voice jolted him awake.

It took a moment for Dalton to get his bearings. He wondered why his head was on the bar, and worse than that, how long had it been there?

He opened one eye when Courtney flipped the overhead lights on, which he thought was kinda rude being that he'd obviously been asleep.

"What the hell?" Dalton grumbled, now lifting his head up and through sleep muddled eyes tried to focus on the Budweiser clock over the cash register.

"What the hell indeed," Courtney replied, pressing a button to release all of the bar sales for her shift. "You feeling okay, Dalton? You were passed out for about an hour and a half. That was after you got several standing ovations for your singing," she finished with a laugh.

Dalton ran his hands through his thoroughly disheveled hair. "What the hell are you talking about Courtney?" he asked gruffly.

"Oh so you don't remember, huh? Well you must've plopped fifty bucks into the jukebox tonight. You had yourself quite the memorial dedication to Harlan and his family, Country Blues style as they say. I swear, you've missed your mark as far as careers go, Dalton. You put the likes of Billy

Dean, Tim McGraw, The Notting Hillbillies and Alice in Chains to shame there buddy. You were wailing those blues. I told Clarence the owner we should book you here sometime. You sure had the tears flowing with your song picks," she finished, emptying the cash register, and putting the bills in piles to count.

"Shit, don't remember a damn thing," Dalton replied, "Hope I didn't make a fool out of myself."

She scoffed. "Were you not listening to me? You were fantastic. Hey, you're in no shape to drive, Dalton. Why don't you go on into the men's room, splash some cold water on your face, take a leak, and by that time I should have the money counted and tucked away in the safe. I'll drive you home."

"Yeah, whatever," Dalton replied, "I guess I do need to wake myself up a bit. Got any coffee made? What the ever loving fuck got into me?"

She smiled, "About six Jell-O shots from what I recall, and funny you ask, I brewed a fresh pot about thirty minutes ago. How do you like your java?"

"Black is fine," he replied, heading towards the Men's room, "and Courtney, thanks."

∞

Twenty minutes later, Dalton was sitting in the passenger seat of Courtney's dilapidated Impala, humming the melody of 'Feel Like Going Home," and intermittently singing some of the lyrics as she drove the deserted road heading east.

"Lord I feel like going home, I tried and I failed and I'm tired and weary. Everything I ever done was wrong, and I feel like going home ... "

"You sure do sing that one good," Courtney said, glancing over at him as she turned down a side road that was not in the direction of Dalton's motel. "You played that one the most on the jukebox tonight. Got some special meaning to you or something?" she asked.

"Naw," Dalton replied, "Just fit my mood I reckon. Or maybe fit the occasion, I don't fucking know. Hey, this isn't the way to my motel," he said, glancing over at Courtney, "What's up, Courtney? You planning on taking advantage of me in my current state, woman?" he asked with a husky laugh.

Courtney laughed along with him as she pulled her car into a trailer park and drove around, parking in front of what Dalton guessed was her place. "Not hardly, Dalton," she said shaking her head. "I just need you to come on inside so you can sober up and then listen to what I've got to say to you. Do you think you could do that for me?"

Dalton was puzzled by her words. But he wasn't sure if it was because he was still buzzed, or because those words were totally out of character for Courtney.

He liked Courtney and all. She'd always been nice to him. But now he wondered if maybe she was coming on to him and she wanted to make sure he was down with it.

Hell, Dalton thought to himself, he'd been celibate since coming to Briar County. That in and of itself was a spectacular feat when he thought aback about all the tail he used to nail regularly.

Courtney was good looking and he remembered her telling him her age. Yeah, he was down with doing a chick a few years older. He could probably still teach her things she'd never imagined in her wildest dreams.

He chuckled aloud.

"What's funny?" she asked, opening the door of her car.

"Just wondered if you've got some ulterior motives here, girl," Dalton replied, climbing out of her car, tossing her a lop-sided grin.

She shook her head, climbing the few steps up to her mobile home and unlocked the door. "Be careful, I have a cat and I don't want you startling her so shut the door quickly behind you in case she gets spooked. She has a habit of darting outside when a stranger comes in here."

Dalton followed her instructions as best he could in his still somewhat inebriated state. "All good," he said laughing, "No pussy gets by me," he finished, giving her a wide grin.

She shook her head once again, spooning coffee into her coffeemaker and filling it with water, flipping the switch to start the brewing process.

"I'm gonna go to my room and get out of these clothes. They stink like the bar. Take a seat, Dalton, I'll be back in a minute."

Dalton sat his ass on a bar stool at the kitchen counter, wondering if Courtney was going to reappear in some short little silk nightie to kick start her seduction moves, but then chuckled at his own male ego delusion because Courtney had never given him a second look. Perhaps he'd lost his touch.

He was still feeling like a fucking failure; still feeling the grief of a family slaughtered, and maybe fucking those feelings out of himself would be exactly what he needed.

He saw a black and white cat scurry from behind the sofa and run back towards what he presumed was Courtney's bedroom.

He got up from the bar stool when the coffee finished brewing and found two ceramic mugs in the cupboard over the sink. He filled both mugs and raised his up to his mouth, taking a sip of the hot brew as Courtney came back out into the living room area, wearing a thick pink terrycloth robe, securely belted shut, and a pair of fuzzy bunny slippers on her feet.

Dalton did a double take when he saw her change of wardrobe, which definitely did not denote ulterior motives of a sexual nature. His surprise did not go unnoticed by Courtney.

"Relax, Tiger," she said, grabbing her mug of coffee, and spooning some sugar into it. "I'm sure you would've rocked my world but that's not why I brought you back here."

Dalton took his seat back on the bar stool and watched as Courtney sat across from him at the breakfast bar. She kept her place neat and clean and furnished nicely.

"So, why did you bring me here, Courtney? I'm not that loaded . . . well, at least not now."

"No worries, babe. I have a feeling your ego will survive." She stirred her coffee with a spoon, a thoughtful expression passed over her face before she spoke again. "Dalton, I've known you since Harlan first brought you into the Peak, months back. I know he was in some ways your best bud, even though you two weren't cut from the same cloth, not even close," she said with a wry smile. "But I have to say, you're not to blame for any of this, so you need to lose the guilt. It's weighing heavy on you, and there's still work to be done here."

Dalton's head shot up at her words. What the hell was that about? For once in his life, Dalton was totally dumbfounded. He ran a hand through his disheveled hair, wondering if he was still under the influence of those moonshine Jell-O shots he'd apparently done earlier in the night.

"Relax," she said, sipping her coffee. "You haven't blown it yet."

"Damn it, Courtney," Dalton growled, "What the hell are you talking about, girl?"

"I'm talking about you and the way you've been moping around with that hang dog look on your face since the murders. You're wearing your D.E.A. affiliation like a prison tattoo."

Dalton nearly choked on the sip of coffee he'd just taken when her words sliced through the air between them. His jaw dropped and his eyes narrowed as he waited for more.

"Yeah, I know. But I haven't known all that long, and of course, you weren't supposed to know that I knew. But the truth is Dalton, I just can't continue watching you like this, and potentially putting everything at risk."

Dalton lowered his head into his hands, massaging his temples, the dull onset of a killer hangover headache starting to throb. "You . . . you're D.E.A?" he asked gruffly. "What the hell? Is this some sort of game that Jack cooked up? If so, why?" Dalton was pissed. And he felt he had every right to be damned pissed!

"Chill, Dalton," Courtney said, "I'm not D.E.A. I'm B.C.I. and before you go getting your shorts in a knot, it isn't absolute protocol for me to be filled in on that being I'm a local. Actually, a local who at one time was convinced you were part of the opioid problem in these parts. Which obviously was because I hadn't been given a heads-up before you rolled into town.

"I was born and raised around here. I probably would've left a few years back, but thanks to our A.G., who is determined to nail the Mexican cartel, I stuck around out of some misplaced streak of civic duty my Mama and Daddy instilled in me, God rest their souls."

Dalton scoffed. He was so damn sick of all the Mexican cartel chatter that was rampant once again with the Hatfield murders. He shook his head. "The dude is so fucking clueless," he snarled. "Mexican cartel had nothing to do with this shit. Not the murders anyway. This wasn't a hit job. This was too up close and personal."

Courtney got up from her barstool, refilling her coffee mug. "Yeah, you know that, I know that, but the powers that be in this state are hung up on their theory. They have a narrative like every damn politician these days and they won't let it go. We cleared the county of the cartel back in 2013. At least for the grow operations. But that didn't seem to satisfy the A.G. He's hung up on that stale old narrative and fails to consider the reality of what's really in place here. This ain't about weed. Seems like everyone's afraid to tackle the opioid crisis. Makes ya wonder, doesn't it?"

"Then you get that none of this was about a weed grow operation, right?" Dalton asked with a sigh of relief following.

"No shit, Sherlock," she replied testily. "Hey, I'm sorry. I don't mean to come off so flippant, it's just that I feel like I've been spinning my wheels here, and I've been at this for more than two damn years. All I keep hearing is to keep my ear to the ground, nose to the air and get those nasty cartel members who are growing pot. Hell, I make more in tips at the Peak than what this undercover gig is paying."

"So wait a minute," Dalton said slowly, "Are you saying your BCI gig is the sideline?"

She smiled at Dalton. "Well, that's a nice way of putting it Dalton, but yeah, paid informant. That's how I got the 4-1-1 on you. But not early on. Nope, you did well up until the murders. But since then, I noticed the change in your demeanor so I figured you were either in on it or you fucked up an assignment. I had to call my contact in Columbus who said he'd get back to me and to lay low."

"And?" Dalton prodded.

"And the night before the wake, the guy in the designer shades and dark suit came up to me in the bar and had a brief chat with me. Didn't tell me anything other than you represented the white hats. I drew my own conclusions after that."

"Jack," Dalton remarked with a pensive smile, "Yeah, he sure as hell looked out of place. I was surprised he showed up at the wake. He's not too happy with my work on the assignment. I feel like I must've really fucked up. Still waiting for my walking papers."

Courtney walked around the bar and gave Dalton a pat on the shoulder. "You need to stop being so hard on yourself. We all knew Harlan and the family had pot growing, but it hardly seems worth the lives of eight people."

"Agreed," Dalton murmured.

"And even though I haven't had the training you've had, I have lived in these parts long enough to know that none of this went down because of pot. This shit was up close and personal. I think you're in a position to bring it to light, Dalton.

"I'm racking my brain Courtney. Kicking my own ass wondering what the hell I missed? I'm not at liberty to divulge anything I know, which at this point, isn't much, but you do understand that, right?"

"Yeah, yeah. I wasn't even supposed to let on that I knew your cover. I was told to leave it alone and let the Big Boys handle it now that they've swarmed onto the scene. But that doesn't give them any advantage over you in my opinion. I mean think about the months you've spent down here, the interactions you've had with folks, things you've learned that might've seemed inconsequential at the time."

"Don't you think I have been, Courtney?" he snapped. "It's fucking all I can think about."

Courtney sighed, "Don't sell yourself short. I'll help anyway I can. But here's the thing you have over me, Dalton, You've got the objectivity that the locals, including me, don't have. Put on your thinking cap and watch others instead of having them watch you. I have faith in you. Fuck the white shirts. They don't know how things roll here in Briar County. You do."

Dalton gave her a smile. "Thanks, Courtney. I guess I needed that. And until I hear different, I'll get my shit together and stay down here, doing what I've been doing. If I'm lucky, I'll piece this twisted puzzle together and maybe, just maybe bring some justice to Briar County. In the meantime, can I crash on your sofa?"

"You've got it," she replied with a smile. "Let me get you a pillow and blanket," she said going to a closet and pulling them out. "And don't worry, I'll keep my killer kitty in my room for protection."

Dalton chuckled as he sat on the edge of her couch and removed his boots and shirt. He stretched out on her sofa, punching the pillow until he'd gotten it just right and pulled the blanket up over his belly.

Courtney was right, he knew that. He was wearing his damn guilt that really wasn't his to own. If he wanted to do right by Harlan's family, he knew the answers were right here in this county.

Not Mexico.

Dalton thought some night fishing might be in order.

WHERE THE CRAWFISH SWIM

Chapter 22

It was three days of night fishing before Dalton managed to catch a break and find Billy Ray Jensen on the bank of the river, his pole in the water, in the darkness of the night.

Dalton had begun to wonder if Billy Ray was in hiding for some reason. His truck had been in his driveway each evening when Dalton had passed his house on the way to the river, and he knew he could've simply stopped at Billy's house for a chat, but that would've been out of character for Dalton. And Billy Ray would've picked up on that.

Dalton knew if he was to get any information out of Billy, it had to be by means of a casual run in, as in the past when they were fishing.

"Hey Billy," Dalton called out as he got closer to the bank. He didn't want to startle the older man who appeared to be deep in thought. "Fish biting?" Dalton asked, dropping his gear to the ground beside Billy's chair, and setting up his own.

"Huh? Oh . . . no not too much but I've only been here for about twenty minutes or so."

"What kind of bait you recommend?" Dalton asked, trying to re-establish their fishing rapport. It'd been a while since they'd last talked.

"Crawdads," Billy replied, but didn't elaborate any further than that, which was unusual.

Dalton baited his hook with the earthworms he'd dug up earlier, and dropped his line into the river. They both sat there in silence for about ten minutes when Dalton finally broke the silence.

"You okay, Billy?" he asked. "Do you want me to move on down the river a piece? It seems like you'd prefer to fish alone this evening. I guess I shouldn't have just presumed you wanted company."

Billy turned and looked over at him. He had a tortured look on his face, and Dalton knew immediately that something indeed was sitting heavy on Billy's mind or perhaps on his conscience.

"Naw, it's not that, Dalton," he replied, "I just . . . I just can't process what happened to the Hatfields, is all. I mean they were my damn neighbors. How did I not see or hear anything that night? It feels weird talking about it to you," he continued, "I mean you being the one who found them and all. I can't imagine what that did to you."

"It's something that will never be erased from my mind, Billy," Dalton said solemnly. "But there's something that keeps sticking in my mind."

"Yeah? What's that?" Billy Ray asked after a quiet pause.

Dalton felt a tug on his line and started reeling it in. "It's just that I was surprised I didn't see you at the wake for the Hatfields, Billy. Seems like everyone else in the county, and then some, were there. But didn't see you."

Dalton reeled the carp in, removed the hook from its mouth, and tossed the fish back into the river.

"You know," Billy Ray commented, "Lots of folks around here consider carp good eatin', Dalton. If you cut out the mud line just right, it fries up nicely."

Dalton re-baited his line and tossed it back into the water. "Maybe so, Billy. Guess I'm a bit picky though, never did develop a taste for bottom feeders. Seems I heard you say that a while back when you hooked one. Have you had a change of heart?"

Billy Ray dropped his pole and turned to face Dalton. "Something you want to say to me Dalton? What is it? Do I owe you an explanation for not attending the funerals of my neighbors? What? You think I'm involved in it some way?"

Billy Ray's voice had risen in anger, and Dalton knew he'd hit a nerve with that one, which was exactly what he'd intended to do. "Didn't say that now did I?" Dalton replied, chewing on a toothpick he'd just pulled from his pocket.

Billy Ray reeled his line in, and started putting things back into his tackle box. "You know Dalton, seems to me that you were way more involved in whatever it was the Hatfields were doing than anyone else around these parts. Seems funny you getting all suspicious about me not being at their funeral. What does that prove? It's been my experience that often times the guilty party is the first one to point fingers at others. And you did, after all, come up on that crime scene first now didn't you?"

Dalton didn't allow himself to react to Billy Ray's thinly veiled accusation. He knew it was simply a tactic to put him on the defensive, and an obvious over-reaction on Billy Ray's part for a question that was mostly benign.

"Whoa, hold up Billy," Dalton said calmly, "I sure didn't mean to imply anything, it just surprised me is all. No need to get your dander up. I'm sure you had your reasons, buddy. No judgment on my part, I'm sorry."

Billy Ray visibly relaxed, and sat back down in his chair, burying his head in his hands, his fingers rubbing his forehead. He shook his head, and looked back up. "I didn't mean to get all worked up about your question, Dalton. I guess maybe I do feel guilty. The truth is, I just couldn't bring myself to go. It's complicated as hell. It doesn't help that the whole county has been nothing but a circus ever since then. I can hardly stand to even leave my place. If it's not FBI field agent or BCI officials, or reporters getting in your way, it's those damn nosy people coming to the county looking for bloodstains on the pavement. You know they're planning on hauling all those mobile homes off the Hatfield property into some old deserted factory over in Scioto County, didn't you?"

"Yeah, I know what you mean," Dalton replied softly, "and no, I wasn't aware that was going to happen. How'd you find out?"

Billy shrugged his shoulders and leaned over and searched for a different lure in his tackle box. "Heard Sheriff Richards talking about it to Ella Johnson earlier when I went in to get some fresh bait. They want to preserve the crime scene. Makes sense I guess. Leaving those mobile homes sitting out there on Hatfield land is just an invitation for thieving and break-ins. This is a high profile case. It's national news."

"You bet your ass it is," Dalton replied, "but you haven't said why you feel guilty about it, Billy. I don't know you well, but I do know you're ex-law enforcement and seem to be a law abiding and solid citizen."

Billy sighed deeply. "The thing is, I only did what I thought was right - right for the community, you know?"

Now Dalton had Billy Ray where he wanted him. He'd been carrying around guilt because he'd gone to someone with his concerns and speculation. Dalton needed to know who exactly that someone was.

"Yeah, Billy, I get it. You're a stand-up guy, who's probably seen a lot of quid pro quo shit during your career. It's hard to know who to trust sometimes, isn't it?"

Billy nodded.

"Remember when you told me you'd raised your concerns about the Hatfields to somebody who you felt you could trust? Who was that, Billy?"

Dalton watched as Billy Ray's face contorted into something that was akin to pain mixed with shame. He waited patiently for a response, hoping like hell Billy felt like getting it off his chest.

"Wasn't anyone in law enforcement around here, Dalton. I don't trust any of them in this county. I believe I did the right thing."

"Was it authorities over in Scioto County?" Dalton pressed, hoping like hell for a name. He knew Billy was at his most vulnerable point; he didn't want to appear overly aggressive in getting that name.

"I'm not saying anything more about it Dalton," he said, now pulling in his line and preparing to gather his gear up to leave. "It's not that I've got you pegged as being a bad person, it's just that right now, anything I say carries risk. This county doesn't need anyone else being put at risk. I'll be seeing you around."

ANDREA SMITH

Chapter 23

It had been over a month since the murders of eight members of the Hatfield family, and law enforcement was still crawling through the back roads, cornfields and woods looking for God knows what.

True to the word around town, all of the mobile homes and double-wides had been moved off the property and put into an empty warehouse in the next county.

Jack had only met with Dalton once at their usual meeting place in Augusta. It had been a week prior. Jack let Dalton know that the hydroponic poppy plants had not been located in any of the searches in the area.

"You're officially no longer a person of interest in that," Jack assured him.

"You know Jack, it's pretty fucked up that I ever was if you want to know the truth. So what am I supposed to do now? There's no more planes coming in, no sign of the hydroponic poppies, and eight dead people. What's my next assignment? I'm spinning my wheels here. I'm supposed to keep my cover, but for what? I receive no intel briefings from you, no instructions of any kind. I appreciate the paychecks, but I'm thinking my services to the D.E.A. might be of better use on another assignment, don't you?"

Jack cleared his throat seeming to be at a loss for words. "I'm afraid it's not that simple, Edwards. You see, in the mind of the A.G. the murders were a direct result of that marijuana grow operation they had going. The Hatfields were stepping on the cartel's business—maybe not in Briar County, but

159

definitely in Appalachia where they've had a stronghold for decades and a supply chain carefully structured to remain beneath the radar. The Hatfields were interrupting that supply chain, and drawing too much attention to the area."

"You've got to be shitting me, Jack. You know damn well that's a bunch of horseshit and we've got proof of that!" Dalton hissed in anger.

Jack's face contorted in anger, and his voice grew hoarse with his next words. "Pipe down and listen to me, dammit! We have nothing," he spat. "Pictures of poppies, video of a Cessna landing and taking off? Unidentifiable people? That Cessna could've been carrying fucking fertilizer for all the proof we have. You blew it Dalton. I'm afraid this is the end of your tenure with the D.E.A. effective immediately."

"Are you serious?" Dalton snapped. "So all of this—it's what? Just going to be shoved under the rug so it looks as if a crime's been solved with no arrests? What the fuck, Jack?"

Jack shook his head. "It wasn't my decision. I'm just the messenger. Your credentials have been revoked. You'll get eight weeks of severance pay, and your laptop has been wiped and disabled. I'll need to take your phone and I.D. with me when we leave. I'm sorry. It was Munson's decision. I guess he didn't have the balls to communicate this to you directly."

Dalton stood up, tossed his government issued cell on the table, and then grabbed his wallet and pulled his D.E.A. identification from underneath the leather flap where he'd kept it hidden. "There you go, Jack. Tell Munson to stick them both up his ass."

And with that, Dalton walked out of Jerry's Restaurant and headed back to Briarton, trying to figure out just what his next move would be in finding a career other than shoveling shit and feeding the exotic animals at the East Fork Ranch.

Chapter 24

"How about another beer, Courtney?" Dalton asked, sliding his empty mug over to the edge of the bar.

It was late afternoon; he'd just gotten off work at the East Fork Ranch and had pulled into The Peak for a cold beer or two. The place was practically deserted, but Dalton knew in a few hours, it would be buzzing with the regulars who came in on Friday nights to blow some of their paychecks.

"Another draft?" she asked, pulling a fresh frosted mug from the cooler.

"Let me try that dark IPA you got in," Dalton replied, getting up to put a buck into the jukebox to play a couple of tunes.

"Sure you can afford it?" she asked with a smirk.

"Ha ha," Dalton replied, choosing two Alan Jackson tunes and a Garth Brooks number. "No worries there, if I get low on money I'll just move onto your couch."

She laughed and poured the dark brew into the frosted mug. "Fat chance. My cat would run you out. But seriously Dalton, what are you going to do?"

He'd filled Courtney in on his termination last week after he'd returned from Augusta. She'd agreed it sucked, but said she wasn't surprised.

"Oh really?" Dalton had challenged, "So you think I'm a loser and botched this whole bit?"

"Nope, didn't say that," she'd replied, "You were set up to fail Dalton, and anybody with half a brain would've done their due diligence before sending a not-quite-outta-the-rookie agent down here. What I'm saying is the asshats in Columbus and every other damn capitol city in this country as far as that goes are conveniently clueless while a good deal of them line their pockets from lobbyists and cartels to look the other way. And that goes for the D.C. bitches as well."

"Wow," Dalton had responded with a big wide grin, "Tell me how you really feel, Courtney."

"Earth to Dalton," Courtney said, bringing his thoughts back to the present. "What's your plan, darlin'?"

"I'm in no hurry to leave. I know that may sound strange, but I've got my severance and I'm sticking around for a bit to nose around. I don't want to leave feeling like a loser. I owe it to myself. And I owe it to the Hatfields."

"You closing the bar tonight?" he asked as she wiped down the outside of the cooler.

"Naw, thank fuck, I'm off at eight, why?"

"Care if I stop by? Now that I've officially had that prison tattoo removed, I'd like to share notes with you. Might help getting some insight from you."

She was thoughtful for a moment, and then nodded. "As long as you know that it goes both ways."

"Absolutely," Dalton replied, taking a swig of his beer. "Between the two of us, maybe we can bring some light to the darkness in Briar County."

Chapter 25

Dalton was busy mixing feed for the horses in the main barn, his thoughts going back to the previous night when he'd both shared information and gleaned information with Courtney, when Duel came up behind him.

"How's it going Dalton?" he asked, startling him. "Whoa," he laughed, "you must be somewhere else boy. Didn't mean to startle you like that."

Dalton turned and ran a gloved hand through his hair. "Naw, it's all good Duel. Was just singing a song in my head that's all."

"Hmm," his boss responded, "Usually enjoy listening to those songs you belt out. Got a real good voice on you. Don't keep it inside, we enjoy the entertainment around here. Especially now with all that's happened," he finished, shaking his head.

"Yeah, you got that right. Anything new with the authorities? I heard the Sheriff is under review or some shit like that."

"Oh yeah? Where'd you hear that?" Duel asked quizzically.

Dalton didn't think it'd been a secret. Courtney had told him that the night before, and she'd heard it at the bar from one of the county deputies. "Heard it at the Peak the other evening," Dalton replied nonchalantly, "Figured you probably already knew about it."

"Nope, but it doesn't surprise me either," Duel replied, "That whole department needs to be dismantled and re-built.

You know they've had more than one deputy who was on the take if you know what I mean."

Dalton did in fact know what Duel meant. It had been one of the topics of discussion he'd had the night before with Courtney. In fact, Dalton had learned that the cop Vince Hatfield purportedly had in his pocket had left the force just days before the murders. Dalton wondered if Vince had even been aware of it. It might have explained that deputy reporting to the local news media that the department was preparing to serve search warrants at the Hatfield property on the same morning Dalton had found them slaughtered.

Then Dalton had shared something with Courtney she hadn't known, and wouldn't have known because Billy Ray Jensen was a teetotaler and never stepped foot inside of The Peak. He was gone. His livestock was gone, his truck was gone, and the house had been emptied out. There was a "No Trespassing" sign nailed to a tree in his front yard.

"Are you serious?" she'd asked, her eyes widening in surprise? "What spooked him? He's been a fixture in this county like - forever!"

"You okay, boy?" Duel asked, bringing Dalton back to the here and now. "Something troubling you?"

"No . . . uh, I guess I was just thinking about what you just said about the local authorities. You know Billy Ray Jensen told me more than once he didn't trust law enforcement even though he came from that world. I'm just a bit antsy like a lot of the folks around here. And now with Billy Ray disappearing ..." he allowed his voice to drift off to silence, not finishing his thought because he really didn't have the words to explain them. He closed the lid to the grain bin and faced Duel. All

Dalton knew was that he had no plausible explanation as to why Jensen would have fled the community where he'd lived all his life, and left in the manner which he did. Quick and unnoticed.

Duel burst out laughing at Dalton's last statement. It wasn't quite the reaction he expected.

"Dalton, boy you must have a flair for the dramatic! Billy Ray didn't *disappear*!" he said, still highly amused.

"No?" Dalton replied, arching an eyebrow in question.

"Naw, he's been looking to relocate for a while now. Asked me if I was interested in buying his livestock and his farm. Actually he sold them to me at a price below market value. Said he had a family situation and needed to relocate to be closer. He moved on over to West Virginia. His older brother lives over there and recently lost his wife, and then took ill. Billy said he felt he was needed there, and hell, he was tired of farming. I can understand his need for a change. I actually did him a favor by taking that place off his hands. It was too much for the old fella," Duel explained.

"Oh yeah?" Dalton replied, "Didn't know he felt that way. Course I guess I didn't know him as well and you and your family did. But do you really need more land than you already have?" It wasn't really any of Dalton's business, but he felt compelled to ask.

Duel chewed on a toothpick and straightened up from where he'd been leaning against a post in the barn. "Well, I couldn't very well pass it up at the price he was asking. Besides, I'd like to grow more crops for feed, and with the additional livestock I bought, they'd feel right at home there. The way I see it, the bad rap this county is taking at present, not only statewide, but also nationally, Billy would've likely had to wait years to sell at a fair price. Add to the fact that his property borders the Hatfield massacre site, I think he wanted to cut his losses and run. Can't much blame him for that."

Dalton nodded, "Yeah, makes sense I guess. But where are Billy's goats and sheep now? Do you want me to handle their care?"

"Thanks, but not necessary Dalton. I'm pasturing them over at the boys place near Pebbles for right now. They've got plenty of room over there and it's already fenced in. Won't hurt either one of them to take on some more responsibilities. They won't have to drive clear into Briarton in order to pasture them, and facing all the BCI agents still hovering around is unsettling for the whole town. In fact, I think it might be therapeutic for them at this point in time."

"That right?" Dalton asked, quirking a questioning brow. "Is Brant having a hard time with this? I mean being a single dad full-time and all?"

"You could say that," Duel remarked. "Sally Jo's keeping Maddie most of the time for now, but the truth is, he's tore up mostly about that newborn baby boy of Tammy's."

"Why's that?" Dalton asked. "Does he think the boy is his?"

"Damn right he does," Duel replied, anger evident in his voice. "Those two, for whatever reason, just couldn't leave one another alone. Problem is, his name isn't on the birth certificate like it should be. That . . . loser James Barton's name is on it. We're gonna have to fix that."

Dalton scratched his head in genuine confusion. He remembered something that Harlan had said which was very similar to what Duel had just shared with him. "Yeah, Harlan said the same thing as you just said, Duel, about Tammy and Brant. Wouldn't that be some crazy shit if it turns out you're right about that? But I have to ask, are you saying that baby's name is Barton Barton?" Dalton asked with a grin.

"Hell no," Duel snapped. "That's another damn reason we believe Tammy knew Brant was the father. She named that baby Barton Hatfield. What does *that* tell you?"

Frankly, it was proof of nothing as far as Dalton was concerned. Wives didn't always take their husband's surnames anymore; babies born out of wedlock were named to suit the mother's fancy. It could be Tammy wanted to appease James Barton that the baby was indeed his, and the fact she was still a Hatfield made the name combination a good fit. "So how you planning on fixing it, Duel?" he asked.

"Already in the works. Ma's lawyer has filed a Motion for DNA testing for the baby in order to establish true paternity. That baby should have what is rightfully his."

Dalton couldn't argue with Duel's statement, but something inside told him the meaning of his words might just go both ways.

ANDREA SMITH

Chapter 26

Monday morning found Dalton Edwards walking up the steps to the Briar County Courthouse in Waverly. Specifically en route to the Probate Division. Something Duel had mentioned the other day about Tammy's infant son deserving *what is his.* Ordinarily, Dalton would've presumed that meant the McCoy fortune. But for some nagging reason he wasn't convinced that was Duel McCoy's true intent.

Once in the clerk's office, he jumped on one of the available computers, and pulled up the docket index. He typed in Vince Hatfield's name and saw that an inventory had been filed and approved by the judge just a couple of days back. He pulled up the inventory list and saw the only things listed were the various automobiles he had on the property used for demolition derbies. That seemed strange to Dalton what with all the land, buildings and livestock the Hatfields owned.

Dalton pulled up the document that was titled Fiduciary Appointed and scanned the dock to see that apparently the family attorney was serving as Fiduciary, and another attorney had been appointed Guardian ad Litem over Tammy's two babies until paternity was established for both.

He shut down the computer and walked up to the desk where one of the clerks gave him a flirty smile and asked, "Can I help you?"

"Yes, Ma'am," Dalton replied, giving her his signature smile. Her nametag read 'Debbie.'

"So Deb," he said, "I wonder if maybe I can see the files on a probate case. I checked it out online, but I wonder if access to the actual files might provide further details, I mean, if that's allowed," he finished.

"Well sure thing. Do you have the case number?"

"I do," Dalton replied as he handed her the scrap of paper where he'd written down the case number and her breath immediately hitched. "Oh my," she said, "That was certainly a tragedy, wasn't it? Are you family?"

"Not by blood, but I was good friends of the Hatfields. I was just a little curious about the inventory of the estate. Nothing listed but those demolition cars. Seems strange."

She nodded, standing up and turning to walk back to where the file room was located. Dalton couldn't help but notice her short skirt and long legs. And he could tell she enjoyed showing off her body by the way she walked, swinging her hips from side to side.

She returned just a couple of minutes later, and motioned for him to step inside the swinging gate where she'd taken a seat at a desk, placing the manila folder in the center. "Take a seat. Let me see if I can't untangle some of this for you," she said tossing her hair behind her back and blessing him with another flirty smile. "I'm no expert, but I think by going through some of the attorney's filings, I might be able to clarify the present situation."

She pulled out some papers from the attorney who was assigned as fiduciary and quickly scanned it. "Okay, see here?" she asked, placing the paper in front of Dalton. It was on the attorney's letterhead. "This here says that Vince Hatfield made arrangements with his personal attorney appointing him as fiduciary of his estate upon his death. That's not all that unusual. Keeps the family members from feuding with one another. Believe me, I've seen some horrific feuds take place. By having a neutral and objective professional handling the details, it really minimized that risk. Now it also looks as if Mr. Hatfield wanted a minimal amount of his property to go through Probate, which does take a lot of time, and can cost more money. So he didn't die intestate. He had a will . . . see here?" she asked, pushing a stapled stack of papers that had Vince's notarized signature and that of his attorney over to Dalton.

Dalton scanned through it and saw that Vince had put his land, buildings, farm implements, livestock, bank accounts, life insurance policies and automobiles titled in his name into Payable or Transferable Upon Death in equal shares to his surviving spouse followed by surviving blood related next of-kin in succession with his blood children first, then blood grandchildren, followed by blood brothers, sisters, nieces and nephews to follow after that. Surviving blood grandparents and then cousins were at the bottom of the inheritance totem pole.

"So Deb," Dalton said, "It looks like Vince Hatfield had a pecking order for his estate so he could avoid the Probate process on most everything, is that right?"

"Exactly," she replied smiling.

"So Debbie, let me ask you this: what's with this Guardian Ad Litem deal with his two grandbabies? I know for a fact that the oldest girl, Maddie, has a father who pays her support and has a relationship with the child. Wouldn't he automatically get custody?"

"Well, the way it works is when there are minor children involved in a . . . situation like this . . . the county automatically appoints an outside attorney to act as G.A.L. just until they sort things out."

She leafed through a few more papers. "Oh, I see here that there's been a DNA blood test ordered for the newborn baby. Apparently there was some doubt raised by a non-family member who wishes to determine paternity of the youngest child and has petitioned the court to order it. That can happen when the child is under two years of age."

Dalton nodded. It all made sense now. Duel McCoy was determined to find out if Maddie would inherit one hundred percent of the estate, or possibly have to split it with Barton's next-of-kin.

He stood up and held his hand out to Debbie to shake it. She placed her hand in his, giving it a playful squeeze.

"Thank you Debbie," he said, "You've been an incredible help with this."

"Anytime," she said with a wink.

"Could you point me in the direction of the County Recorder's office?" he asked.

"Sure thing. Take the elevator up to the third floor, and it's the second door to your left after you step off."

Dalton found his way there, and once again pulled up property transfer files for the county. There it was. A quitclaim deed executed a week after the Hatfield murders transferring Billy Ray Jensen's farm to Duel McCoy for the sum of $60,000. The signatures were notarized by Sally Jo McCoy. Dalton paid a buck for a copy of the deed and headed out, his mind churning with possibilities.

As Dalton walked back down the steps of the Probate Court, he now knew that Duel McCoy was a person of interest.

And, despite the fact that Dalton was no longer an asset of the D.E.A. he was not giving up on getting to the bottom of the Hatfield massacre.

After all, he still worked for Duel so he was in a prime position to observe Duel's activities. Whether he was an active participant, or covering for his sons, or both, Dalton was determined to find the truth. And the first truth he needed to find was something other than the copy of the quitclaim deed folded up in his pocket to compare the signature of Billy Ray Jensen to another public record that could be made available.

Chapter 27

Two days later, Dalton was back working his shift at East Fork Ranch, watching as Duel seemed to be pre-occupied with non-ranch issues. He'd been in and out all day, doing business errands and going to appointments he'd explained to Dalton.

"Things are a might busy around here what with being shorthanded," he explained to Dalton. "The boys need me to lend a hand over at their place for a bit, so I'll need you to take charge over here, Dalton. Are you up for it?" he asked.

"Absolutely," Dalton replied, "Anything you need done, just make a list and I'll see to it, Duel. So the boys are busy, huh?"

"Yeah, got their hands full with the livestock and some crops coming in. Thanks for stepping up for me here. I'll be back around three or four. If you could get the horse trailer cleaned out and washed up, put some fresh straw in it, check the tires and air them up if needed that would sure help me out. I'm taking them to the vet in Lexington tomorrow morning."

"I'll do it," Dalton assured him. "Do you need me back here tomorrow to help you load them up, Duel?"

"No need. I'm leaving pretty early. Just come by around nine or ten o'clock and clean out their stalls, put out fresh feed and water before I get back. Grant's going with me, and Brant is working at their place all day. Just take off when you're done. Oh, and I appreciate your coming in on one of your off days to help out."

"No problem, Duel. I'll handle it. No worries."

∞

Dalton got his normal chores finished and then started on the horse trailer. Duel generally took a dozen of the Falabella miniatures at a time to the veterinarian down in Lexington. Apparently, they needed monthly check-ups to make sure their blood tests showed no abnormalities that might require a change in their feed mix or vitamin shots, Duel had once explained. Then two weeks later, Duel would take the rest of them to the vet to go through the same damn thing.

To Dalton, it seemed like these tiny horses were extremely delicate creatures and he hadn't seen too much breeding activity taking place, at least for as long as he'd been working at the ranch. But then, he was only there three days a week so he could've missed all the *horseplay* days. He laughed out loud at his own thought. The truth was, he didn't really know shit about horses, big or little.

Once he finished up, he was done for the day and took off heading for The Peak. He'd given Courtney a copy of the quitclaim deed, and asked if she could find a way to dig up something else with Billy Ray Jensen's signature. She assured him she'd be on it.

He pulled into the parking lot and was glad to see the place wasn't packed yet for happy hour. The bar was deserted, with just a sprinkling of patrons over in the booths, watching a baseball game on the flat screen.

Courtney came bustling around from the back, carrying a tray of clean beer mugs for the cooler. "Well hey there, Dalton," she greeted. "Thought you'd be in a little earlier."

Dalton took a seat on one of the empty stools, tapping his palms against the surface of the bar. "Had some extra duties today," he replied, watching as Courtney stacked the mugs inside of the cooler. "Got any frosty mugs left?" he asked with a grin.

"Sure do, your favorite IP draft?"

"Absolutely."

Courtney drew him the dark draft and placed it on the bar in front of him. She glanced over at the other customers to make sure they were staying put before she pulled a folded packet of paper from her back jean pocket and handed it over to Dalton. "Check it out," she said quietly.

Dalton unfolded the papers. One was the quitclaim deed copy he'd given her, the other was an index card for Billy Ray Jensen's voter registration. It was the original.

"How the hell....?" he started as he glanced at the signature and seeing they didn't come close to matching one another.

"Don't ask," Courtney replied with a snicker. "Let's just say I have a lot of respect for Wilma Styer still working at the Briar County Board of Elections at the age of seventy-seven what with her incontinence issues and all."

Dalton gave a chuckle. "I can make a copy of this if you want to sneak the original back into her files," he offered.

"I don't think that will be necessary," Courtney replied, "It's all online, that's how I knew Jensen was registered to vote, but I needed to see the actual card he signed to see his signature. Besides," she continued, "I don't think Billy Ray will be votin' around here anymore. I don't think Billy Ray will be votin' at all if you want to know my opinion."

"Whoa, slow down Courtney. This is at best, something we can have analyzed by an expert in handwriting for forgery, but it's a stretch to say it proves murder."

"Find the body," she quipped, "I'd bet a year's worth of tips he's dead. And tell me, now that you're 'persona non grata' with the Feds, how will you get these signatures analyzed?"

Dalton took a long draw of his beer. "Courtney, Courtney," he said, giving her a grin, "I have resources. Never doubt that I have my ways," he finished with a wink.

"Of that I'm sure," she replied shaking her head. "Keep me posted."

WHERE THE CRAWFISH SWIM

Chapter 28

Dalton left the bar and made a quick phone call to Jack from his new phone. He wasn't sure Jack would answer a call coming in from an unknown number, but only agency colleagues had this number so he was hoping that'd be enough. Turned out that it was.

"Yeah," Jack answered, not identifying himself just in case his number had been leaked.

"Jack, it's me . . . it's Dalton," he said quickly, "Listen I've got something for you."

There was a momentary pause. Dalton could hear Jack sigh on the other end.

"Edwards," he said, "You're not on assignment anymore, hell, you're not even on the payroll anymore. We aren't having this conversation."

"Hold up!" Dalton said loudly, "Trust me, Jack, I'm not looking to be reinstated, but I've got something that you're going to want to see and I don't trust this with anyone else, so what does that tell you? I'll need ten minutes of your time. Then if you want to tell me to fuck off and lose your number, I will."

Another pause. Another sigh.

"I can meet you in Augusta day after tomorrow. It'll have to be early evening, say seven o'clock?"

"That works for me," Dalton replied. I'll see you then Jack."

Dalton returned to his motel and pulled out his new laptop, quickly going through search records to get some sort of an electronic footprint of Billy Ray Jensen, knowing that the chances of that were slim to none. He couldn't picture Billy Ray surfing the web, tweeting, face-booking, or putting selfies out there.

People Search did shed some light on his basic information. And some relatives were listed, but Dalton knew sometimes those named were skewed by living at the same address, in-laws, etc. Still, there was a name listed, Clarence Jensen listed as a relative, in his early seventies, living in Welch, West Virginia.

Dalton pulled up a map of West Virginia and had a helluva time finding Welch. He finally found it in the southeastern part of the state, not all that far from the Virginia state line. Damn, the population was 2400 at the last census, and it was situated in coal country. Probably just as poverty-ridden as Briar County. Dalton looked at Mapquest and saw that it was a four-hour drive from Briarton to Welch.

Dalton then found the McDowell County website, only to find they did not offer online property records. Shit. Was he surprised? Not really. He dialed the phone number listed on the website and got a recording that the county offices were closed and would re-open the following day at eight o'clock a.m.

He'd call first thing before going out to East Fork Ranch. He had a gnawing feeling in his gut that Courtney was likely on to something, and he wanted that piece of information before he met with Jack in two days.

Chapter 29

Dalton was up by seven the next morning, showering shaving and getting dressed in clean work clothes. The summer was hot and humid. He got away with wearing a white sleeveless tee and jeans. He was glad he would be outta there by noon when the day turned into a furnace until late afternoon.

At eight sharp, he called the McDowell county offices again, this time a live person answered the phone. Dalton asked for the recorder's office and was quickly transferred over.

"County Recorder, this is Fern McMillan, how can I help you?"

"Yes, Fern, my name is Dalton Edwards and I'm calling from over in Ohio. I tried to check your land records online, but unfortunately, they aren't available which is why I'm calling."

"Mr. Edwards," the woman cut in, "If you want copies of deeds, liens or what-nots, you'll have to come in and pay $3.00 per document copy. We don't take credit card payments, Paypal or Checks. It's cash on the barrel. This is a poor county and we just don't have the means to give out information or copies for free, you hear?"

"Ma'am," Dalton said nicely, "You see, here's the thing. I'm trying to locate somebody. It's a next-of-kin type situation, and I'm not even sure if this person owns his home. I simply have a name and a street address. So you see, I'm not looking for a copy of a deed, a lien or a what-not, I just figured Welch being a small town, you might be familiar with the individual I'm trying to locate. The name is Clarence J. Jensen, and the address I have is on Mud Hen Road in Welch."

The words were barely out of Dalton's mouth when he heard Fern's gasp and quick intake of breath.

"Ms. McMillan, are you okay?" he asked.

"Oh . . . uh, yeah, give me a second here," she rasped. "You took me by surprise with that one," she said. "Mr. Edwards, Clarence Jensen has been dead for five or six years now. He and his wife were killed when their house burnt plumb to the ground. They were lovely people. It was just a shame, yes it was. They had no children. Word around town was that Edna was barren, so it was always just the two of them. Devoted to one another like a husband and wife should be, you know?"

Dalton wasn't sure why Fern McMillan was giving him all this additional information, but he was going to take advantage of her knowledge of the Jensens.

"Can I ask you why you're looking for next of kin?" she asked.

"Well, I'm trying to locate Clarence's younger brother. He's missing. His name is Billy Ray Jensen. Ever heard of him?"

"Hmm . . ." she said slowly, repeating the name. "No, I don't think I ever met a brother. Can't recall Clarence or Edna ever mentioning one either. I'm sorry I can't help you, Mr. Edwards. But that's all I know."

"Thank you Fern," Dalton replied, "You've helped me more than you know. Have a great day."

So there it was. More unraveling of the Duel McCoy story on Billy Ray Jensen.

∞

Dalton checked the horse barn as soon as he arrived at the ranch. It was only eight-thirty but it looked as if they'd already left. There were only eight of the miniature horses left inside. It seemed to Dalton that Duel should invest in a larger trailer instead of having to make two trips a month clear to Lexington.

He was hosing out the empty stalls and had just put fresh straw down when his cell phone vibrated in his back pocket. He wiped the sweat from his brow and grabbed his cell.

It was Courtney.

"Dalton," he said swiping the screen.

"Hey," Courtney said, "You're at the ranch right now aren't you?" she asked.

"Yeah, what's up?"

"Elroy Driscoll just called me at The Peak while I was getting ready to open up. He asked if I had your cell number, said he saw your truck at the McCoy's and he wants you to call him when you get a chance. Said it's private."

"Sounds ominous," Dalton replied. "The family isn't here. It's just me today, and it looks like Virginia is out as well. Do you have Elroy's number?"

"Sure do," she answered, "I'll text it to you when we hang up."

"Sounds good, Courtney. I'll give him a holler. Thanks."

"Let me know what's going on," she said, "He really sounded as if it was important."

"Will do."

Dalton filled up the feed and water buckets and when he heard the ping on his cell, he pulled up Courtney's text message and dialed up Elroy.

"Hey Elroy, it's Dalton. What's up?"

"Dalton, " he said, his voice was clearly on edge, "I didn't want to come onto McCoy property to fetch you, but you've got to come over to my place now. There's something here you've got to see for yourself. I'm in my garage. The overhead door is shut, so come in through the side door. Hurry."

Dalton jumped into his truck and drove out of the ranch down the road about a quarter of a mile and pulled into the gravel drive leading up to Elroy's garage. Once the truck stopped and he shut off the engine, Elroy had the side door of his garage opened, and was beckoning for Dalton to hurry up on inside.

Dalton had no clue as to what Elroy had inside of his garage that had put him into such a panic mode, but once he stepped inside, he saw the cause of Elroy Driscoll's distress.

"Holy hell," Dalton breathed, "how in the hell did this horse get over here, and what the hell is wrong with him?"

It was obviously one of the McCoy's tiny horses, but clearly, the animal was suffering with some sort of illness. He was lying on an old blanket, and Dalton could tell it was one of the older horses. The animal seemed to be having convulsions, unable to stand, his head was moving from side to side, and he was foaming at the mouth, snorting and making sounds that were foreign to Dalton.

"I tried to make the poor thing comfortable. Do you reckon he's rabid?" Elroy asked.

"I don't see how that could be," Dalton replied, squatting down next to the animal to get a closer look. "Duel has them to the vet for check-ups and shots monthly. How did this one get over here?"

"I don't know for sure. I saw Duel and one of his boys pull out earlier this morning with the trailer hitched up to their truck, and about fifteen minutes later, while I was working on a car, this one here comes a staggering into the garage. Snorting and foaming at the mouth. I got a blanket down and put it on the floor for him before he collapsed. That's when I saw you pull into the ranch. I figured I needed to let somebody know."

As Dalton watched the animal calm, the foamy liquid still spilling from his open mouth, a prior conversation Dalton had had with Jack months back suddenly popped into his head.

"*. . . the courier had swallowed fourteen heroin pellets and one had ruptured inside of his intestine. He was foaming at the mouth, so his handler calls down to Mexico to find out what to do . . . told him to cut the courier open and retrieve the remaining drugs.*"

"Fuck!" Dalton growled. "It's not rabies, Elroy. This animal is couriering drugs in his gut. Something went wrong."

"Huh?" Elroy said, his forehead creased in confusion.

"Listen Elroy, I need your help. We've got to get this animal to a veterinarian, but it can't be anyone local. It has to be someplace where people won't know the McCoys. We *have* to keep this between us, trust me on this, it is very important."

"Ida's nephew Dennis. He's a veterinarian assistant for a guy down in Grayson, Kentucky. But that's over an hour away. Do you think the horse will make it that long?" Elroy asked.

They both glanced over at the horse, who had calmed somewhat, but his breathing was labored. "He's not going to make it Elroy, but what's important now is to establish what caused this and have it verified and on the record by a qualified vet who doesn't know the McCoy's. Can you call him? Let him know I'm coming in, but nothing else. And I'll need the address."

"Sure thing," Elroy said, "give me five minutes." He left the garage and headed up to his house.

Dalton turned his attention back to the horse, who no longer seemed to be in any pain or distress. He wrapped him up in the blanket, and carried him out of the garage, quickly depositing him into the bed of his truck.

Once he'd secured the bed cover, Elroy was back, and handed Dalton a piece of paper. "I called Dennis and let him know you were bringing a miniature horse in that likely had expired. I told him you could be trusted, and to do what he needed to do in order to find out the cause of death."

"Thanks, Elroy."

As Dalton was climbing into the truck, Elroy reached out and touched his shoulder, causing Dalton to turn back to face him.

"Dalton," the older man started, "if they find drugs in the horse, what's to say they can pin it on the McCoy's and not you?"

"I'm hoping to have someone meet me there who can establish I'm not a person of interest in this. You have to trust me on this, Elroy. You and Ida's safety could be at risk if you share what happened today with anyone, do you understand?"

Elroy swallowed and gave Dalton a firm nod. "You did something for us Dalton that saved my home and my livelihood. Ida and I will always be grateful for that, and you have our trust unconditionally. No worries on that. We won't tell a soul. Good luck, son."

Dalton plugged the address into his GPS and hit the road, giving a voice command to "call Jack." The phone rang several times, and Dalton prayed Jack picked up. He breathed a sigh of relief when he did, and Dalton told him he had in his custody one of the mules for the drug smuggling in Briar County.

"What the hell are you talking about, Edwards?" Jack barked. "You don't have the authority to arrest or detain! Are you fucking crazy?"

"Jack, I don't have time to explain it all. If you want the goods, meet me at this address. I'll be there in approximately an hour, and your ETA should be close to that. It's worth your time, Jack. I promise."

ANDREA SMITH

Chapter 30

Jack Reynard was taking a chance in going out on what could be a *career-ending* limb if his superiors got wind of it. He jumped into his car, putting the address Dalton Edwards had given him into his GPS.

The truth was, Jack thought the agency had given Edwards a raw deal. The D.E.A., like any government agency, was plagued with layers of bureaucracy, political leanings and autocratic leadership. Jack had been around long enough to realize the tactics and strategies put in place in cities like Chicago, New York or L.A., weren't conducive to achieving results in places like Lewiston, Illinois, Paducah, Kentucky or Briarton, Ohio.

The agency hadn't adapted their strategies to accommodate the new and developing intricacies of the Rural America drug supply chain. The cartels were widespread focused on small town networks that were more difficult to detect.

Jack knew that Dalton had done his best, and had, in fact, blended well into the community and maintained his cover under some of the most difficult circumstances in such a clannish small community.

His GPS informed him that he had reached his destination as he pulled into a parking lot of an animal clinic.

What the hell?

When Edwards had said he was in custody of a drug *mule*, he hadn't taken that word *literally* for Chrissake!

He shook his head and chuckled as he got out of his vehicle and headed inside of the clinic.

Right away the receptionist ushered him back to a hallway, and opened the door for him to enter one of the examination rooms.

"Jack, glad you made it," Dalton said, turning to introduce him to Dr. Kincaid, Doctor of Veterinary Medicine, and his assistant, Dennis Richardson.

"We waited for you before beginning," Dalton explained, moving to the side where Jack could see what appeared to be a tiny horse, no bigger than a large dog laying dead on the stainless steel examining table. Jack looked back quickly at Dalton, his brows furrowed in confusion.

"What the..?" he started to blurt.

"Jack, Dr. Kincaid needs to see your D.E.A. credentials before he begins his examination of the carcass of this recently expired Falabella Miniature, found wandering at a residence in southeastern, Ohio. It is my belief that the animal has been packed with some type of illegal narcotics, similar to the incident which occurred some months back in Lorain, Ohio if you recall?"

Jack immediately knew exactly the incident Dalton was referencing. *'Son of a bitch'*, he thought. What better way to transport without drawing suspicion than this? Jack didn't need to be told the name of the owner, he knew exactly who it was, and it was smart of Dalton not to bring names into mixed company.

Jack dug out his badge and handed it over to Dr. Kincaid to confirm.

"Thank you, Agent Reynard," Kincaid replied handing it back to him. "This is going to be easy to extract. If you look at the X-Ray we took, you can see clearly that a plastic tube of some sort had been inserted rectally into the animal."

Kincaid flipped a switch so the X-ray panel lit up and pointed to what clearly looked to be a cylindrical tube containing pellets of some sort inside the tiny horse's lower intestine. With your permission, I'll remove it now," he continued, slipping on latex gloves.

"Go ahead," Jack replied, taking out his cell and pressing the camera button to record the removal of the foreign object. "I'm ready."

∞

"Are you sure you want to assume this risk, Edwards? You realize I can't sanction this with the agency. You're not—"

"I know, I know Jack, I'm *not* on the payroll. I'm *not* an agent, I get it. But the proof we got inside that clinic doesn't do squat for snagging the network, plus, there's still the matter I explained to you on the Billy Ray Jensen situation."

They were both standing outside in the parking lot of the clinic. Jack Reynard had taken a couple of the pellets retrieved from the plastic cylinder to confirm it was heroin, but Dalton Edwards had little doubt it was anything else. And he knew exactly the source of this recent batch: the missing poppies. It had to be.

"Now finding proof that this ... *Billy Ray* has been murdered is a stretch. Yeah, it sounds like Duel McCoy gave you a fake story, but it could be Billy Ray was scared off and chose to sell out and go underground," Jack argued. "But listen, I *will* have these signatures analyzed," he conceded.

"Thanks, Jack. Well, it's noon, so I need to make tracks back to the ranch. If time's on my side, I can get this carcass back behind one of the barns so they think he wandered off and died without anybody being the wiser. Since Kincaid put that tube back inside of the horse, they'll surely think their secrets are safe. Wonder if they knew before they left that the plastic tube had cracked and the poor damn animal was overdosing?"

"Hard telling," Jack said with a sigh. "Collateral damage they'll try to minimize in the future I expect. Be careful, and Dalton? Keep me posted so we can be prepared for the next trip to whatever veterinarian they've got in Lexington who's helping them mule this poison."

"You've got it."

WHERE THE CRAWFISH SWIM

Chapter 31

It had been over a week since the big reveal as to how the McCoys were up to their eyebrows in heroin trafficking using their Falabella miniatures, through a veterinarian in Lexington. Dalton had remained mum on the subject, not even sharing with Courtney what he and Elroy Driscoll had discovered. He felt bad about keeping her in the dark, but this operation was too critical to take even the smallest risk of a leak.

Dalton had maintained his usual demeanor at the ranch, and in fact, the following day when he had returned to work, Duel asked him if he'd mind digging a grave for one of the miniatures they'd lost.

"Sure," Dalton had replied, "What happened, man, they all seemed okay when I was with them yesterday morning?"

"Mollie-Belle was old," Duel had said, his demeanor solemn as if the loss of this animal tugged at his heartstrings. "She must've got loose from the rest and wandered out back. Grant found her in the field behind the barn. Old animals do that, you know? It's their time and they sense it. They kinda put themselves out to pasture to die."

"I'm sorry, Duel. I know how much the miniatures mean to you and the family," he lied. "I'll get to it right away. Where do you want her grave?"

Dalton didn't doubt that Duel or Grant had made sure to pull the broken plastic cylinder, containing the rest of the heroin pellets out of the horse's ass as they paid their last respects to poor old Mollie-Belle.

Since that time, Dalton had kept his senses on high alert, keeping track of the comings and goings of the various family members. The boys hadn't been around much at all, which was unusual, but only confirmed what Dalton suspected: They were busy harvesting and processing the poppies they'd stolen from the basement of Vince Hatfield's marijuana grow operation. In his mind, he was trying to figure out how in the hell Duel had gotten wind of it at all.

Was it possible that Billy Ray Jensen had known more about the Hatfields operation than Dalton had given him credit for? Had Billy Ray been the person instrumental in having those search warrants issued the very morning the massacred bodies were discovered?

There hadn't been a Cessna delivery for two months prior to the murders . . . so where was Duel now getting the raw materials for the heroin pellets?

Dalton knew in his gut where he was getting it, and that the boys were busy processing it over at their place near Pebbles.

Dalton was finishing up his chores when Duel came out to the barn smiling, which was indeed rare.

"You gonna give me congratulations on my new grandson, Dalton?" he said, holding out his hand for Dalton to shake it. Duel laughed heartily at the obvious cluelessness of his ranch hand. "We got the DNA results back. Barton Hatfield is officially Barton McCoy! It came back 99.89%. Doesn't get much closer than that, right?"

Dalton gave Duel's hand a hearty shake. "Well yes sir," he replied, "Congratulations to you and Brant. I'm glad you're so happy about it."

"Happy?" Duel asked excitedly, "Happy isn't the word! I'm totally unabashedly thrilled with the good news. You don't know how the not-knowing has just eaten us all up these past couple of months. Now we can finalize our plans."

"Plans?" Dalton asked. "You mean a big celebration or something?"

"Naw, nothing like that. Now that paternity has been established, the Guardian ad Litem is out of the picture. Sally Jo and I promised Brant we'd help him take the kids, the horses and start their own ranch somewhere away from here. Maybe Tennessee, Alabama or Arkansas - hell, maybe even Alaska, dammit!" He clapped his hands together in happiness. "It's just a huge weight off of all of us. We're sick and tired of all the publicity that's been given to this county and our little town. We need a break, we fucking deserve to walk into town without people gawking at little Maddie, or giving Brant the hairy eyeball as if he somehow is to blame. It's just too fucked up around here."

"So, will you be back, Duel? Or should I be looking for another job?"

"Naw, no worries there, Dalton. Sally Jo and I will be back just as soon as we get Brant and the youngins settled. Sally Jo's already been on line checking out land for sale in Tennessee, Alabama and Arkansas. We don't want them too far away. So don't worry about looking for work. I'll still have some of the horses, and hell, I've still got the pigs, peacocks and thinking about getting some exotic birds as well. Besides that, it seems that it's gonna take a while to get the estate settled what with Maddie and Barton being the Hatfield next-of-kin and all."

"Oh yeah?" Dalton asked as if he hadn't already known that through his visit to the county court office, "Didn't know that. Well, I guess that's double congratulations to you then. Seems like you've inherited a bunch of land to farm or ranch."

"Right?" Duel said still grinning like the greedy fool he was, "So you've definitely got job security. Probably will need you full time before long, so you stay put, hear?"

"Sure thing," Dalton replied returning the smile. "Looking forward to it Duel."

WHERE THE CRAWFISH SWIM

Chapter 32

The Beginning of the End.

It was a week and a half after Duel's announcement that Dalton found himself sprawled out on the sofa in the living room of Courtney's trailer, catching all kinds of hell for holding out on her the way he had.

"I thought we were in this together, you rotten mother-fucker," she said, her voice raised in anger. "So much for trust, huh?"

"Courtney, c'mon sweetheart, I told you *now* didn't I? Don't you think I'd have told you before now if I could've?" Dalton asked, his voice contrite.

"Oh bullshit," she said, taking a swipe at the side of his head. "Don't you think you can charm your way out of this, you aren't even with the agency anymore, so you had no code of conduct to follow. Give me a freakin' break!"

She went over to the fridge and grabbed a bottle of beer. "You want one?" she asked grudgingly.

"Only if it means I'm forgiven," Dalton replied sheepishly.

"Oh save it, whore dog," she said with a laugh, "you're forgiven, so give me the deets again. This is so damn exciting."

She uncapped the beer and handed it to him as she took a swig of hers and settled in the recliner across the room from him.

"Okay, so it's all going down tomorrow. Duel and Brant are headed down with the horses to their veterinarian connection in Lexington. Somebody has attached a GPS monitor under the trailer and the truck."

"Hmm," Courtney said snickering, "Wonder who the hell would've done that? Continue please."

"So the Kentucky State Police in cooperation with the D.E.A. will be in unmarked vehicles along the way, tracking their movements to the destination in question, keeping in contact with one another. Once they are in place, and the animals have been offloaded into the veterinary clinic, they will officially be served with search and seizure warrants and taken into custody."

Courtney squealed, pounding her feet against the seat of the chair. "That is so awesome, and then what?"

Dalton took a swig of beer and then gave her a grin, "Well, back at the ranch, or should I say ranches," he said with a chuckle, "there will be D.E.A. and B.C.I. agents simultaneously serving warrants to Sally Jo McCoy, Virginia McCoy, and Grant McCoy at their respective residences, along with some drug sniffing and cadaver dogs for good measure."

"Do you really think Billy Ray Jensen is dead?" she asked sadly.

"Yeah, I do. The way I figure it, is that he was too close to blowing the whistle on the Hatfields, which presented a major problem for the McCoys. My guess is that when Vince refused to lease or sell that land to Duel, he figured out that Vince had a gig of his own going that was way more lucrative than hydroponic pot. He made it his mission to find out just what that was.

"After the murders, Billy Ray knew that Duel or his sons or maybe all of them were a part of it. He realized he'd trusted the wrong damn person in Briar County. He was ridden with guilt. He might've even reported his suspicions to somebody at the Sheriff's office. But poor old Billy Ray just didn't know how many cops Duel had in his pocket."

"So," Courtney said, "Is that why Duel made it look as if he'd bought Billy Ray out?"

"Yep. My guess was Billy Ray was already dead so he got rid of his truck, his body, and had that quitclaim deed forged and notarized by Sally Jo. What a stupid fuck."

"But what if they don't find a body? They can't prove murder without a body?"

Dalton nodded. "It would purely be circumstantial, but it can be done. We'll just have to wait and see."

"And what are your plans for tomorrow Dalton? I mean while all this shit is going down?" she asked.

"Me? Well, it's my day off. I guess I'll be hanging out with you at The Peak."

"Uh huh," she mumbled giving him an eye roll, "and to make sure I don't have loose lips, right Dalton?"

"C'mon Courtney, let me off the hook here, babe."

"Well, as long as you keep me posted after it all goes down."

"No problem. But I think this will be well-publicized when the dust settles."

ANDREA SMITH

Chapter 33

After the dust settles . . .

Once again the town of Briarton, Ohio was crawling with local, state and federal law enforcement agents. All patting themselves on the back for local television crews, the Attorney General giving live press conferences articulating as to how the various agencies worked tirelessly and intelligently to snag a major transport ring of heroin, meth and cocaine tied to the Espinosa cartel.

The national headlines were reporting that six members of the McCoy family were arrested on various charges including twenty-two counts of murder in connection with the 2016 Hatfield family massacre, two counts of capital murder for the abduction and murder of local resident Billy Ray Jensen, whose charred bone fragments were found in a burn barrel on the property owned by Brant and Grant McCoy. Additional charges of obstructing justice, abuse of a corpse, drug trafficking, drug possession, possession of drug paraphernalia, forgery to commit fraud, child endangering, tampering with evidence and animal abuse were issued against various family members including Sally Jo McCoy, Duel McCoy, Virginia McCoy, Grant McCoy and Brant McCoy. Two minor children were taken into custody of Children's Protective Services pending the arraignment of all family members.

Dalton Edwards sat at the bar at The Peak, watching the news reporting on various cable networks.

Courtney placed a frosted mug of beer in front of him. "It's on me, Dalton," she said, "for a job well done, although to hear all those talking heads, sounds to me like they're taking credit for doing squat. Makes me wanna puke."

"I'm not sweating it, Courtney," he replied, "Knowing the internal politics within government agencies, I wouldn't have expected anything less. It's political posturing for the upcoming elections."

"Still," she said, furiously wiping down the bar top, "If it wasn't for you, they'd all still be sitting on their thumbs, pointing their fingers at one another. You get no recognition for any of it, forgive me if it pisses me off."

"It's just as well, Courtney," Dalton said, grabbing a pretzel from the bowl she'd set in front of him and munching on it, "The judicial system is just as fucked up as the rest. It will take months, if not years for them to untangle all of the players, the motives, the evidence, all the while hoping that the McCoys will start ratting one another out in an attempt to muddy the already shit-filled swamp."

"No doubt about that," she agreed, nodding her head. "So, what's your theory, Dalton. I'd love to hear it."

Dalton popped another pretzel into his mouth, and chewed thoughtfully. "Well, I think several things might've been at play here. I think Duel got wind of Vince Hatfield's secret poppy operation, which more than likely originated with Billy Ray Jensen's involvement. You see, the way I figure it was that Billy Ray went to Duel and entrusted him with the knowledge he had of the drug trafficking activities, along with the identification of those two black Suburbans. Billy Ray was thinking it was the Hatfields, which proved to be his fatal mistake in the end."

"The thing is," Courtney cut in, "why in the world did Billy Ray go to Duel and not the cops?"

"That's easy," Dalton responded, "Billy Ray had a general mistrust of all law enforcement based on a career's worth of seeing officers on the take. In Briar County, there seemed to be an over abundance of it, and I'm positive that Billy Ray was the one who finally convinced the Sheriff's Department to get warrants issued for search and seizure of the Hatfield property.

"If Vince had a cop in his pocket, Duel probably had three of them. So obviously, that information got to Duel McCoy in advance. It gave him and the boys time to plan the execution of the family. The way Duel figured it was that Vince was squeezing him out of the opioid business, which likely had ties to the cartel. But Duel was smart enough to know Vince wasn't doing it because he planned to double his hydroponic weed operation. That wouldn't have netted him the monthly lease fee he was getting from Duel for the landing strip. Duel *had to* conclude that Vince was squeezing him out of the business to go solo on higher revenue narcotics: cocaine, heroin, synthetic opioids -whatever. That was the breaking point."

"But how could Duel have known about the poppies? You said you only found them by sheer accident."

Dalton took another swig of beer. "Remember I told you about those half-moon shaped bruises all over Vince's head and torso?"

Courtney nodded.

"Well, I do know that when they searched Duel's property, they confiscated a pair of leather cowboy boots that had metal heel plates in a half-moon shape from one of his barns. It tested positive for Vince Hatfield's DNA."

"No shit?" Courtney replied.

"My thinking is that he initially beat the information out of Vince, kept him hog tied until the others verified the poppies, and then proceeded to execute the whole family, giving them plenty of time to load up those poppies and take them over to Brant and Grant's place. It solved their immediate problem with keeping their part of the supply chain going. More than likely they traded the bricks for some finished product in order to continue the transport to Lexington and beyond. It was an interim solution until Duel could get his hands on the land and start landing Cessnas again. He wasn't about to alienate the cartel and disrupt the flow of product to their ultimate destinations in this part of the country."

"So," Courtney said, "by executing them and making it look like the Mexican cartel had actually made the hit, it gave the McCoys an opportunity to inherit the Hatfield land holdings since the next of kin were Tammy's two babies?"

"Exactly," Dalton replied, "and thus putting the landing strip back in business."

"And Billy Ray?"

"I think Billy Ray saw the light after the massacre of the Hatfield family. I figure he either threatened to blow the whistle on Duel, or refused to sell his property to him. Either way, Billy Ray had become a liability Duel just wanted out of the picture."

"Man," Courtney replied, letting out a hard sigh, "Who would have ever thought the McCoys would be involved in something this huge?"

"Oh, I think my first clue was when I saw how much Virginia McCoy was worth. Over $5 million in this neck of the woods? Plus her land contract schemes showed her true nature more than any of those so-called benevolent non-profits she used as a tax shield. Hell, before it's all over, the IRS will probably have their hands in this as well."

"It sure sounds as if the McCoys won't see the light of freedom for a long, long time, Dalton. And it's all thanks to you whether those government dick heads want to admit it or not."

Dalton gave her a warm smile. "I appreciate your sentiments, Courtney, and I've really enjoyed working with you behind the scenes, but remember, everyone - including the McCoys - are innocent until proven guilty. That's the law of this great land. And it's what sets this country apart from a Banana Republic."

"You're right about that, Dalton. And I hope it never changes." She wrapped her arms around Dalton and gave him a hug. "Gonna miss you around here, not gonna lie. Especially your singing. You really ought to consider that as a career."

Dalton gave her ponytail a tug, and lifted her chin with his fingers. "I'll miss you too, Courtney, maybe someday you'll find your way outta here," he said gently, brushing a kiss across her forehead. "You're so much better than Briar County, Ohio, woman."

ANDREA SMITH

Epilogue

Two Days Later . . .

Dalton was busy packing the clean clothes he'd just picked up from the laundromat. Miss Millie, who ran the establishment, had been amenable to Dalton's drop off and pick-up request, only charging him an extra ten bucks for the personalized service. Dalton had always given her twenty bucks nevertheless.

"Heard you're leaving these parts, Dalton," she'd said. "Guess with the Hatfields gone and the McCoys all in jail awaitin' their trials, not much work for you to do. Shame to see you go. We all really enjoyed having you around the community."

"Aww . . . thanks Miss Millie, I've enjoyed being part of this community in spite of all that's happened around here. Quite a shocker."

Millie had put her hand up to her cheek, shaking her head back and forth. "Just unbelievable," she said, "Never in a million years would I expect something so horrible to happen to two of the nicest families in the county. I keep thinking there's got to be more to the story. I keep hoping it's all just a huge mistake."

"Time will tell, Millie. You take care now and thanks for doing such a great job with my laundry over the past year just about."

"Has it been that long, Dalton?"

"Yep, would've been a year this coming January."

"Time sure has flown I reckon. But if you're ever out this way again, you be sure to stop in and say hello, won't you?"

"I sure will Millie."

∞

Dalton took one last look around the motel room to make sure everything he'd brought with him, and stuff he'd acquired since living in Briar County had been packed in a suitcase or boxed up. He'd already settled his bill with the manager. Just as he was getting ready to leave, there was a tap on his door.

When he opened it, he was face to face with Elroy Driscoll. "You're leaving without even saying goodbye?" Elroy asked with a slight grin.

"I was gonna stop by on my way out of town, Elroy," Dalton replied with a wink.

"Like hell you were," Elroy said with a chuckle. "I know why you didn't stop but it doesn't matter, because I told you way back that I would pay you back the money you gave me to keep Duel McCoy from evicting Ida and me."

"Look, Elroy," Dalton replied, "You helped me more than enough to cover that money. Plus, you've kept my secret from the rest of the town, which means a lot. You and Courtney are about the only two people in the county I trust without hesitation."

"Dalton, please take the money, son. I helped you because I knew you would do the right thing and rid this town of the evil that's plagued it and you did just that. I won't take 'no' as an answer," the older man said, holding out a wad of bills.

Dalton reluctantly took the wad, shoving it into the pocket of his jacket. "Thanks, Elroy. You and Ida take care now. Stay safe."

They shook hands and Dalton watched as Elroy got into his truck, waving to him as he pulled out of the motel parking lot.

Once in his truck and on the road, he was singing along to a country tune when his cell phone rang. He hit the button on the steering wheel to answer the call on speaker.

"Dalton," Jack Reynard said, "been meaning to call you. This is long overdue, but I want to personally thank you for bringing the situation in Briar County to closure. I know you've not received the credit you deserve, but you do understand that since you weren't technically—-"

"On the payroll," Dalton interrupted, "Yeah, yeah I get it Jack. It's no big deal."

"Well, it is to me," Jack responded. "I've made some calls. I think I can get you back into the D.E.A. There's some openings in Oklahoma and Nebraska. I personally know the division managers and they're nothing like that idiot Munson you got stuck with in Columbus. I'd be happy to give you a stellar recommendation, that is, if you're interested."

"I appreciate that Jack, but I'm not all that bothered by the lack of recognition. Kind of like being off the radar knowing that I can wash my hands of the Briar County shit. I won't be called to testify as I'm not a material witness to any of the crimes. They've got the DNA from Duel's boot, the smoking burn barrel containing what's left of Billy Ray Jensen, the forged quitclaim deed, the stash of drugs, and before it's over, I'm betting they'll indict the horse veterinarian out of

Lexington. With the Forensic Accounting and Information Technology team, the two burned out Suburbans found buried in the woods at the boys' property in Pebbles, the digital files uncovered from Billy Ray's surveillance camera, I'd say they've got what they need. I don't really want to be a part of the D.E.A. again."

There was a momentary pause in the conversation. Finally Jack spoke up. "What will you do now, Dalton? You've got good skills and intuition. I'd hate to see it not used in your career path."

Dalton chuckled. "No worries on that, Jack. I'm headed to Douglas, Arizona."

"What the hell is in Douglas, Arizona, Edwards?"

"A job I think I can really sink my teeth into, Jack. Under the Department of Homeland Security. A law enforcement position."

"Are you serious?" Jack asked, his voice laced with a bit of shock if not disbelief. "You're going to be an I.C.E. agent?"

"Why not?" Dalton replied with a chuckle. "Our incoming Prez has made a strong commitment to securing our borders, and enforcing laws that haven't been enforced for generations. After what I experienced in one small town in one state in rural America, I can only surmise the extent of this epidemic nationwide. Seriously, Jack, it boggles my fucking mind."

There was another pause, and then Jack spoke up. "Good Luck, Edwards. I think you've made the right decision. Keep in touch though, will you?"

"Will do, Jack."

THE END

WHERE THE CRAWFISH SWIM

Don't miss out!

Visit the website below and you can sign up to receive emails whenever Andrea Smith publishes a new book. There's no charge and no obligation.

https://books2read.com/r/B-A-DYO-RRHZB

BOOKS 2 READ

Connecting independent readers to independent writers.

Did you love *Where the Crawfish Swim*? Then you should read *Dirty Diana*[1] by Andrea Smith!

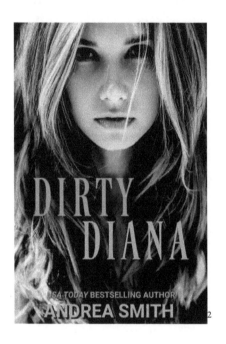

[2]

At sixteen, I felt I would always be a misfit.

Popularity had eluded me, and I was pretty much a loner by choice. My world existed on the internet; gaming, and chat rooms were my escape, because there, my anonymity was my shield.Known by my handle, D-10, I fit in with the others, and met some phenomenal virtual friends. One special friend in fact was Dastardly Damned. We clicked. We gamed online, and finally we made plans to meet at a local hangout.***Only I never saw his face. I never saw what was coming.My life would never***

---

1. https://books2read.com/u/3JjZ0A

2. https://books2read.com/u/3JjZ0A

be the same.And DastardlyDamned would pay... ADULT
CONTENT

Read more at www.andreasmithauthor.com.

Lightning Source UK Ltd.
Milton Keynes UK
UKHW011313010323
417858UK00004B/281